STAY

By Briana Michaels

COPYRIGHT

Dedication

To all the readers
who learn by getting spanked —
I hope your ass is always red
and the Os never stop.

Chapter 1

Cole

"I want you to come all over my face."

Jaedyn gawks at me. "Are you sure?"

I stare at the acronyms again. "Yeah. Pretty sure."

He looks at his cell, mouth twitching. "Damn." His thumbs rapid tap a reply to whoever just sent him that message. "I hope you're right, man."

I punch the floor number on the elevator and stand back against the wall.

His cell dings again and he laughs. "You were right." He smacks my shoulder, excitement lighting his face. "How the hell do you solve these things so fast?"

"One of my many talents, I guess." Jaedyn's been hooking up with some mystery woman for a couple months now, and she always texts him shit like TMTSTFUATYDLAGG, which he has to decode before they meet up again. I have no clue what he gets as a prize for guessing the right answer, but I'm not about to ask.

TMI.

"You ever use an electroshock toy on a woman's clit before?"

Jesus, it's too early for this convo. "Yes."

"You're my hero."

I've dated women who were adventurous in the bedroom. Masks, paddles, floggers, and stimulators are always in my arsenal. I like my woman begging for my cock, because I'll damn sure return the favor and worship her pussy. Wanna be praised, degraded, rewarded, and punished? I got you. Most women suck my dick harder when I call them a good girl, but filthy bitch, cum slut, and pretty little whore also do the trick. And if I hear a woman moan my name, I'll work overtime to make sure she can't walk once I'm done giving her as many Os as she can stand.

I'm a giver like that.

Of all the women I've had the honor of pleasuring though, one stays permanently embedded in my brain.

Haley Davis.

We met in college and had a wild motherfucking senior year together. To say she left an impression on me is an understatement. I compare every woman to her, which isn't fair to anyone. But how could I not? I thought Haley and I were endgame, but I was wrong.

She set the bar high. Probably too high, considering no one else has reached it.

My brother Trey once told me I put her on a pedestal because she was my first and my

4

memory of her is probably no longer accurate.

He's wrong. I remember every second of our time together with perfect clarity.

The ropes. The chains. The beautiful degradation. The scent of her shampoo and the feel of her soft thighs on my cheeks when I'd bury my face in her sweet pussy.

Fuuuuck. I'm getting hard just thinking about it.

Rounding the bend, I walk straight towards the receptionist who smiles at both of us. "Good morning, gentlemen." Tamara swivels in her chair and shoves two coffees at us. "There are donuts in the breakroom too."

"Marry me," I say, just as Jaedyn goes, "I love you."

Laughing, she snags two files from her desk and holds them up to me. "These need to be signed and couriered by noon, Cole."

"No problem."

"Noah's in a mood," she warns. "He's already pissing and moaning about the holiday party."

"Why does he insist on having it every year when he hates doing it?" Jaedyn shakes his head. "No one's forcing him to throw anything."

"It's good for morale and business," Tamara says in her best boss voice. "But yeah, I agree. It's such a pain in the ass and we're the ones who have to suffer Noah's shitty mood while he plans it."

"He should just delegate it out." Jaedyn tips his head at Tamara. "You should plan it."

"Oh hell no." She shakes her head. "I learned my lesson three years ago when I organized a baby shower for my sister. It was so much work I was ready to quit by the time she cut the cake. Besides..." Tamara lowers her voice. "Can you imagine the micromanaging Noah would do?" She shivers dramatically. "I'd die of frustration."

Noah's a brilliant businessman, but he's also a control freak with a temper. He's made more than one employee cry around here. I can't stand the man, but I've put up with him for the past three years because I'm a little stuck with which direction I want to take my career next. In the meantime, the pay and benefits are nice.

Tamara glances at her watch and tips her head towards my office. "You better hurry in there, Cole. Your nine o'clock has been waiting since eight fifteen."

My brow furrows. "I don't have an appointment until eleven."

"I emailed you yesterday saying you had a new client add-on."

Shit. "I didn't see it." Because I didn't look.

I've been on a mission to leave work at the office lately and part of that practice includes not opening my emails once I step foot inside my house.

Tamara scrambles to apologize. "I'm so

sorry. I should have—"

"It's not your fault. This is on me." I'm not like Noah, so there's no chance of me blowing up over something this small. Waving the files in the air as I turn to head to my office, I get my head in the game. "I'll sign these for you in a couple of hours, so you can schedule the courier."

"Thanks!" she calls out.

Walking down the hall, checking my cell, I refresh my emails so I can at least find out the client's name before I step into this meeting. It's moments like this when I wish we had a lobby for clients to wait in. But we're not a doctor's office, we're architects. I usually meet them at their house or business.

Christ. Seventy-six new emails fill my inbox. Half of them are from Tamara. There's no way I can find the one I need fast enough.

Fuck it.

Pushing my glass door open, I stare at the back of a woman's head and immediately think of Haley. It's the curly auburn hair that does it. And the slope of her shoulders. She's about the same height too. An ache forms in my chest because I miss that woman so much that some days it actually hurts.

Okay, I need to pull my head out of memory lane and get down to business. "Good morning. Sorry to have kept you waiting."

The woman turns in her seat, and our gazes collide. "Hi, Cole."

Hot liquid splashes all over my shoes and legs. I think I just dropped my coffee.

I *know* I dropped my files.

I've also dropped my motherfucking jaw.

Haley.

"Let me get that." She kneels on the floor, gathering my things while I still can't move.

I should do something. Say something. Pull her back to her feet at the very least, because having her on her knees like this makes my dick hard. Especially when she looks up at me with those big, blue eyes, and her pretty little pink mouth curves in a sexy grin.

Like she's doing now.

My manners and common sense vanish.

My brain fritzes.

I think steam is billowing out of my ears.

How is she here? How is this real?

"Here you go," she says, lifting my files that are now dripping coffee.

I can't fucking move. Memories override my ability to speak as I'm thrown back to the good times...

"Get on your knees for Daddy." I press my hand against her head and push down. "That's a good girl."

"I need your cum." Haley grips my dick with both hands and sucks on the head like it's a fucking popsicle. "Give it to me."

"Good girls use their manners." Threading my fingers through her hair, I pull it. "Try again."

"Please, Daddy, can I have your cum?" She bats her lashes and my knees almost buckle. I could totally get used to being called Daddy. Her brow furrows as she stares up at me, waiting for me to give her permission to suck my dick. Her sweet pouty voice drops to normal when she asks, "Is the Daddy thing not working for you?"

"Huh?"

"Do you like it or not? I can switch to Sir. Master? Ummm." She pumps my length while pondering what honorific to go with.

"Daddy's good." Really damn good. "Sorry, I fritzed for minute. You just…" I close my eyes and groan when she massages my balls with her free hand. "Shit, that's good."

"You like that, huh?"

"Yeah."

"How about this?" She sucks one of my balls into her mouth and pulls it tight.

My eyes roll so hard they nearly disconnect from my skull. "Oh yeah, that's a winner."

Shit, what am I doing? Shaking my head, I snap out of the memory and help Haley rise to her feet. "I can't believe you're here."

Confusion makes her brows furrow. "I made an appointment." When I don't respond, her cheeks redden, and she grows flustered. "Maybe I should go. I'm sorry, I—"

The thought of her bolting out of my life again spurs me into action.

"How have you been?" I want to touch her,

9

but don't trust myself. Every move, noise, or look she makes will likely drop me back into a memory. Five years after going our separate ways, it only took one second back in her presence to make me feel like it's only been a minute since we've last seen each other.

Why is she here? My heart immediately fills with hope that she's come back for me. That we'll get a second chance. It's crazy, I know, but I can't help it.

She's so beautiful. How is it possible that she's even prettier now than before? "You look…" Words fail me. I'm in so much trouble. "Busy."

Yup. Big trouble. I sound like a douche.

Haley smooths her skirt, as if there's any possibility it would be out of place. The damned thing looks painted on her, displaying the flare of her hips and the delicious curve of her ass and thighs.

"You look *busy,* too." She bites her lip. "Umm. Look, I thought you knew I was coming here this morning, but clearly, I've made some kind of mistake. I'm sorry if I've made you uncomfortable. I'll leave."

My body and brain finally catch up with each other and just as she heads for the door, I beat her to it. "No."

Pressing my hand on the door, keeping it closed, I look down at her. She's five-foot four barefooted, but her heels give her a few inches more. It puts our mouths closer to together.

She smells the same. Sounds the same.

Fuuuuck.

I don't know how to do this. I can't separate past and present. I can't separate business from pleasure.

I can't let her leave.

"Stay," I say in a gruff, unprofessional tone.

Her pupils dilate. Her mouth parts a little.

Yes, Daddy, my mind says in her voice. My dick twitches in my slacks.

I'm going to get fired for sexually harassing a client if I can't find my control. And my office is made of glass.

Much like my heart.

"Let's start over," she suggests, and I refuse to recall how she used to say those exact words whenever we'd explore some new kink or role play scene and one of us fucked up. "Hi, Cole." Haley holds her hand out for me to shake. "Long time no see."

I stare at her, ready to play along, but when she tucks her hair behind her ear with her free hand, something glittery catches my attention.

There's a massive diamond ring on her finger.

My stomach plummets. Every fantasy, every memory, every dream, every hope that this meeting is the universe's way of bringing us back together like some kind of fated second chance romance bursts into flames.

My professionalism slides back into place as my mind goes white with numbness.

I shake her hand like a professional, feeling my heart lay bricks around itself. "How have you been, Haley?"

"Good," she half laughs. It's her nervous giggle. I remember it well. "Really good, actually, which is why I'm here."

While my throat tightens up, I point at a chair. "Have a seat." She obeys while I gather my composure and sit across from her. "Now, what do you need from me?"

Chapter 2

Haley

"What do you need from me?" Cole asks, peppering hot kisses down my body.

"I need you to make me come." Arching my back, I groan as he latches onto my pussy and shoves his f—

Nope. Stop that. I can't be thinking dirty thoughts of the man I'm trying to hire to design my new office. It's so unprofessional and awkward.

And embarrassing.

I gave his secretary my name and said it was important that she relayed it. Did he think some other Haley Davis was meeting with him this morning? Or maybe he's forgotten all about the shit we used to do together.

Either way, he doesn't look happy to see me.

I shouldn't be surprised. We parted ways so coldly back then. As if walking away as fast as possible might make the heartache less agonizing. At least, that's how it was for me.

Who knows why Cole let me go.

You weren't that special to him, Haley. Get a grip and be professional. Don't make this worse.

He asked what I needed from him, so here goes. "I'd like for you to design my new office space." My hands shake when I pull out the blueprints for my new investment. "I have the third floor, but it's not conducive to my business with the way it's set up now."

I hand him the drawings, and he carefully unrolls them on his pristine desk. To my left is a huge drafting table and stool that I'm sure he uses a lot more.

"What is it you do now?" His big hands spread out the paper, and he places weights down to hold the corners in place.

I remember how he used to hold me in place and use those big hands to spread my body, too.

"Ummm. I have a party planning business. Event coordinating, I mean." Oh my god. I sound so stupid. It's just that I'm beyond flustered. Sitting across from the love of my life and pretending like it doesn't faze me is absolute torture.

I want nothing more than to crawl into his lap and kiss the hell out of him.

How on earth did Cole get hotter? Is that even legal?

Cole's eyes snap to mine and a huge smile blazes across his face. "You did it?" He leans in and looks absolutely ecstatic. "You fucking made your big Silver Lining Events dream come true?"

He remembers that?

Don't read into it, Haley.

"Yeah." A giggle bubbles out of me. "But it's not Silver Lining Events. It's Next Level events. You know, like—"

"Bring your wedding to the next level."

He gets me. "Yeah, exactly."

"Nice." His bright white teeth are mesmerizing. As are his full lips. "I'm really proud of you, Hales."

Hales.

Tears threatened to blur my vision and my throat closes up. I didn't expect a flood of memories to hit me like this, nor the emotions that come with it. I thought I was stronger than this.

No, you didn't. It's why you're here. It's why you stalked him on social media and found where he worked.

I moved to Banner Bay about six months ago. Planting my roots in this area is a great start to my biggest dream come true. Well, my second biggest dream come true. The first one burned to the ground five years ago.

I'd love to say it's because the area is growing exponentially, and since I plan everything from educational events to book conventions, holiday parties to weddings, this is a brilliant career move. But that's only half true.

I came for Cole.

While he looks over the old blueprint, I nervously spin the ring on my finger. It's a habit I picked up when I started wearing this gaudy thing a couple years ago and I can't seem to stop.

"It's the old Strathom Building." His gaze flies over the layout.

"Um yeah." I guess. I have no idea what it used to be. I just know it was in my price range and is in a great location.

"What do you have in mind?" Cole asks without looking at me.

"I'd like to have a big office for myself and three or four smaller ones. A common work area too." I dig out another paper from my bag. "Here. Something like this." Embarrassment pokes my pride when I slip my colorful drawing onto his desk. "I was trying to come up with something that's open, but still offers each employee a private space."

I sound like a fool.

Cole runs his hands along my sketch, and I swear I feel it on my thighs. My pussy reacts accordingly.

Then he looks over at the blueprint and shakes his head. "Too many load-bearing walls here." He taps my drawing where I want my office. "Unless we want to spin the layout the other way, but then you lose the windows."

"That's okay." I lean forward to see what he means. "I don't need windows."

"You love the sun." He looks up at me with this expression I can't pinpoint. Adoration? Concern? Fuck if I know. I can't read him anymore, and the realization stings.

Cole grabs a stack of Post-it Notes,

16

scribbling little things and slapping them all over the blueprint. "How about we do a walkthrough so I can see the space, then we'll go from there."

"Sure." I stand up. "We can take my car."

He leans back in his seat. "I mean at another time."

My heart drops. "Oh. Yeah. Right." I scratch my head. "Sorry, that was presumptuous. You're probably crazy busy today. All week. I'm glad you could at least fit me in."

"Don't worry, we'll make it fit, princess." My thighs clench at the memory of him saying that the first time we had sex. Blowing out a long, shaky exhale, I gesture at the drawing. "You can keep that."

Cole's brows knit. His phone rings.

I should go. He's a busy guy and taking up more of his time than necessary would be rude.

Hooking my thumb over my shoulder, I step back. "I'm just gonna go."

He rises from his chair and my God, he's stunning. The black suit is tailored perfectly for his body, and he's gotten way more muscular since I last saw him. Considering he played basketball throughout college, his physique has always been perfection. Now it's just mouth-wateringly unfair to the rest of the human species.

"Two," he says. His phone finally stops ringing.

"Huh?"

"I can meet you at two today."

Relief washes over me, and I don't know why. "Um. Okay. Yeah. Two works." Hell, I'll clear my entire day, week, month, if I have to.

He carefully rolls up the blueprints and shoves them back into the tube. Walking around his desk, he seems powerful, intense. Cautious.

"See you then," he says quietly, handing me the blueprints. When I take it, he clasps his other hand around mine and runs his finger over my diamond. "I'm really happy for you, Haley."

Words catch in my throat.

I step away, desperate to breathe, and grab my bag from the floor. "Two o'clock?"

"I'll be there."

"Okay."

I leave without looking back.

Just like I did five motherfucking years ago.

Chapter 3

Cole

I'm worthless for the rest of the morning. All my concentration has blown out the window.

Why is she here?

Why did she move to Banner Bay?

Who is the lucky motherfucking piece of shit who's marrying her?

Does he love her like I do?

Whoa. I better get a grip. I don't love Haley. I love the memories of what we had back then.

Staring at her color-coded drawing of what she wants for her office space, my heart clenches. She's still sketching out her visions. It was something she did all the time when planning campus parties. Because yeah, she planned them. Like full on themed shit, not just kegs and coolers. They were fucking epic too.

My girl has talent, and she's making a living off it. I'm so proud of her.

She's not my girl, I remind myself again. She's someone else's now. And going off the size of that rock on her hand, he's making bank.

Noah sticks his head in my office. "Hey, where are we with the Campus project?"

"Already submitted." I slide Haley's

drawing across my desk and into my top drawer.

"And the corrections on the designs from Brent?"

Shit. I forgot those needed to be couriered by noon. Annnd I dropped my coffee all over them. "Handled."

"Awesome." Noah knocks his fists on the doorjamb. "You got time to look at the list for the holiday party? We can grab lunch at two and go over the clients who should be invited."

Shit. "I've got an appointment then."

"No, you don't. I checked with Tamara."

I hate that he's a micromanaging busy body. "She didn't know. It was a last-minute add-on."

"Hmmph. Alright." He turns to leave and then stops. "Hey, who was that new client you had in here this morning?"

"Someone looking for a quick floor redesign."

"She's hot."

"She's taken," I say through gritted teeth.

"She can always get taken again," he shoots back. "I mean, goddamn, did you see the size of her ass? There's room for two back there."

My hands ball into fists and I lift off my seat so fast, there's no hiding that I'm about to leap over my desk to throttle the man who signs my paychecks. But I stop myself from following through because I can't afford to lose my job or go to jail for beating the shit out of my boss. This isn't the first time Noah has talked like that about a client. It won't be the last. He's a player who's filthy rich, and he always gets away with his bad behavior.

"You need to watch how you fucking talk about clients, Noah. You're going to get a sexual harassment lawsuit one day."

It's moments like this when I hate myself for working here. The pay is incredible, but the management is fucking embarrassing. It's why I started working on the side with my brother, Trey, redesigning the houses he flips with the love of his life, Erin.

And it's the biggest reason I'll be putting my resignation in right after the holidays. I can't leave before then or I would. But I'm waiting with bated breath to hear back from one last project before I walk out these doors for good.

Noah puts his hands up and laughs. "I was just kidding."

Fuck this asshole. "Is there anything else you need?"

"Nah. You're on top of shit as always."

I stare at him again, and something in me cringes. Noah looks rough. "You've got powdered sugar on your shirt."

He looks down. "Oh shit." He hastily brushes it off. "Thanks, man."

"No problem."

The door shuts softly behind him, and I watch Noah stalk to the next office down from mine. I hate that we're in glass fishbowls. I hate that I can't strangle my boss because murder is wrong. I hate that the company feels like it's gone downhill over the past year, and I don't know why or if the reason is somehow my fault.

"What the fuck was that about?" Jaedyn asks, peeking in.

"Nothing." I sign the coffee-stained papers and brush past him on my way out. If Jaedyn wants to press, he doesn't. I drop the files on Tamara's desk when I get to the lobby and head straight for the elevator.

• • •

Two o'clock hits and I'm standing outside a building, waiting for Haley to show up.

When two fifteen hits, worry creeps in.

Two twenty-two and I'm about ready to leave.

"Sorry!" She runs towards me with a large bag hooked around her arm and two drinks in her hand. "I mis-judged the parking situation big time. I still haven't gotten a permit yet, and had to find a spot on the street, which is a bitch, by the way." She halts right in front of me, catching her breath. "I hope double mochas are still your thing."

I stare at the drink she offers me. "And a filthy chai with extra cinnamon is still yours?" I hold out a cup to her, too.

We've both bought our favorites to give to

each other.

This is trouble.

Haley stares at our drinks for a moment, then giggles. "Oh my gosh, Cole." Her laughter is music to my ears. "Didn't think you'd remember that."

"I can't forget," I confess, not at all talking about her favorite drink. "And thanks." We swap drinks and I take a sip of mine. I haven't had a double iced mocha in years, but I'm not telling her that.

We both two-fist our overpriced beverages up to the third floor.

"Ta da!" Haley saunters into her clusterfuck of an office space.

There are so many walls, it's chopped the whole place up. "What used to be in here?"

"I don't know. I didn't ask. It's been unused for a few years and the price was right, so I took it. The blueprints were from when it was barebones, though, which I'm totally willing to take it back to. We can strip everything and start fresh."

That's a lot of construction work. And a lot of money.

Haley sets her cups on an abandoned desk and drops her large bag on the floor. "This…" she announces excitedly, "is where I want to display pictures of my best events. I've got some killer photos printed and framed already."

I set my drinks down next to hers as she

rushes past me to another closed off area.

Her voice rises with excitement as she says, "I'll have pedestals for cakes and centerpieces over here so that when you first come in—" She spins around and runs smack into my chest. "Oomph."

I grip her arms to hold her steady.

She smells amazing.

When Haley looks up at me, her cheeks redden. "Um. So, anyway." She brushes the hair away from her face. That damned engagement ring taunts me. "Yeah. I'll have a display. And then over here," she says, grabbing my hand and pulling me down the narrow hallway, "is where we'll have big meetings. And I want a loaded kitchen area over there."

"A full kitchen?"

"For sure. With a wine fridge."

"You need a fully functioning kitchen and wine fridge to work?"

Haley's shoulders lift. "I want to offer champagne to my clients if the occasion calls for it. And also, I want to eat. I work long hours and it's cheaper to cook here than to eat out all the time. My waistline can thank me later."

My hand is still in hers. Of its own accord, my thumb runs along her ring again.

I can't think past the fact that someone else has won her heart. Someone else will get to see her happy every day. Someone else is going to kiss her each morning and fuck her every night.

When we parted ways, it wrecked me. I just didn't let anyone see it. After graduation, I went straight into another program to get my master's degree and erased her number from my cell, because the temptation to call her was too much for me to handle. Hell, I didn't even have the strength to look her up on social media because I didn't trust myself to not stalk her.

She wanted a clean break. I made sure she got it.

But now Haley's back in my world, and I hate it. I hate that she's moved to my city. I hate that I'll breathe the same air as the woman I'll never have.

Because I never stopped loving her. It's my biggest secret and right now it feels like my worst toxic trait. She's marrying someone else when it should have been *me*. I'm a glutton for punishment asking this, but I have to know. "Who's the lucky man, Haley?"

"There isn't one," she says so quietly I wonder if she spoke at all.

"*What*?"

"There isn't one," she repeats louder, and her cheeks turn red again. She holds her hand up and that fucking diamond gleams like a disco ball in my face. "This is fake."

I must be hearing things. "Why are you wearing a fake engagement ring?"

"Long story." She pulls away from me and clears her throat. "So anyway, I think over here would be a good place to—"

I spin her around and hold her hips, my eyes boring into hers. Those bricks I've stacked around my heart all day start falling. "You're not engaged?"

Haley shakes her head.

"Are you dating someone?"

She shakes her head again.

"Are you…" Fuck, I can't even ask this next question. It might just put me six feet under if her answer isn't what I want to hear.

Haley stares up at me and bites her bottom lip.

Fuck it. I'm asking. "Why did you come to see me, Haley?"

Her pulse quickens, the vein in her throat fluttering wildly. "I…I um…"

Say it. Say the truth. Put me out of my misery and tell me why you came.

"I need a talented architect."

Bullshit. Any construction worker worth his salt could tell her what walls to knock down and build her what she wants. Going with an architect for a project like this isn't necessary. "Why me?"

"You're the best in town."

Not hardly. But I'm one of them. "You could have gone *anywhere*." My heart beats harder in my chest, making my stomach twist. "Why did you come to Banner Bay, and why did you come to *me*?"

She swallows and looks down at the floor.

Nope. She doesn't get to look away from me. Tipping her chin with my finger, I growl, "*Why*?"

"Because," she says in a shaky voice. Tears well in her eyes, making those baby blues glassy. "I never stopped thinking about you, Cole."

Thinking isn't loving. Loving isn't fantasizing. We've notoriously blurred lines in the past and it's what got us in trouble before. I'm not foolish enough to believe she's going to stay around and plant roots here. Haley runs. She's never stayed in one place for too long. If I get my hopes up thinking she'll stick around, I'm a bigger dumbass than I gave myself credit for.

But for her to say she hasn't stopped thinking about me? *Damn*. I hate that my heart's tripping over itself about it. "You could have just reached out." I step away before I do something stupid like kiss her. "I'm all over social media."

"I know you are," she whispers. "But I wanted to see you in person."

"Why?" I feel like she's somehow tricked me, and I don't like it. "*Why*, Haley?"

"To see if what we had before was just pretend, or…" She looks away from me. "Or if it's really all gone."

She's wrong. It's neither of those things.

When I cup her face and lean in, Haley's chin trembles and the first tear falls.

I break.

Smashing my mouth to hers, I drive Haley

backwards until we hit a wall, then I press against her. Our tongues twirl while our hands run all over every body part we can reach. Before I lose my ever-loving mind, I break away. "Do you have your fucking answer now, *Angel*?"

She gasps.

"Yes." Her shoulders collapse as she presses her hand on my chest. I'm sure she feels my heart kicking.

"Yes, what?" I raise an eyebrow.

"Yes, Daddy."

Holy fuck, we're both in so much trouble if we can fall so easily back into our old ways.

Haley yanks me closer, crushing her mouth to mine, and drives me backwards. I stumble over her bag as we make our way towards the abandoned desk.

She just pulled the pin in my grenade. My control ceases to exist. She's no better. We turn into a tornado of lust, clashing and spinning across her office space. We no sooner hit an object than bounce off it until we slam into something else. The chemistry we had five years ago is nothing compared to how explosive we are today.

I don't know what's happening. I don't know if I want to care either.

She wrecked me once, and I survived. Even if she destroys me a second time, it'll be worth it.

One more minute with Haley is worth everything.

Chapter 4

Haley

What am I doing? What am I doing? WHAT AM I DOING?

I shouldn't have made an appointment at his office like that. I shouldn't have brought him here, either. And I *definitely* shouldn't be kissing him.

But I can't help myself.

I've stalked Cole online ever since the day we parted ways. It's been torture.

But we had an understanding that what we did in college stayed at college. We were young and fresh and had our career paths laid out before us with a ton of goals to reach. Cole's life took him in one direction. Mine took me in the opposite one.

We weren't willing to risk our personal ambitions for anything.

Not even love.

Except I'm not sure he ever loved me like I did him. It's not like I bared my soul to him back then. Hell, I'm not even sure how or when I fell in love with him in the first place. It just happened.

But as good as it was, we weren't supposed to last, so instead of confessing my feelings, I bottled them up.

No biggie. He never once dropped the L-bomb with me, either. We had fun. Lots and lots of fun. But that's it. We were basically just friends with hella amazing benefits.

And even though he treated me like I was special, I always reminded myself that that's how Cole is. He treats *everyone* like they're his best friend. He'd give a stranger the shirt on his back without even being asked. The man would do anything for anyone because he's amazing.

How is he still single?

Wait. Maybe he isn't.

Did I make a huge mistake? What people post on social media is rarely the full picture of their life. Cole might have someone special. Someone he kisses every morning, thinks about all day, and goes home to each night.

A wave of nausea assaults me. Pressing my hand to his chest, I hold him at arm's length. "Are you with anyone?"

He looks at me like I have two heads. "The fuck kind of question is that?" Cole steps back with his brow furrowed. "You know me better than that, Haley."

Of course, he'd never cheat. Cole's loyal to the bone. My heart can't figure out if it's relieved that I may have a chance with him, or sad because no one's claimed him yet. He's the best catch ever.

The one who got away.

No. He's the one I let go.

And I'll be forever mad at myself for it, too. "It's just hard to imagine you're not taken."

His tone softens. "Same could be said for you." Cole's gaze drifts back to my diamond ring.

Maybe he doesn't believe it's fake. Spinning it, because my nerves are a wreck again, I admit my lies. "I wear this so I'm not hit on as much." Wow. That sounds egotistical as fuck. "After I finished my internship in Boston, I moved to New York. My supervisor was a real pig. He'd always make me feel uncomfortable and when I brought it up to HR, they didn't do anything about it."

Cole cusses under his breath.

"So, after a year of putting up with him hitting on me and acting highly inappropriate, I made up a fake boyfriend."

His brow arches. "And that worked?"

"Nope." I tuck some of my hair behind my ears. "My boss didn't care at all. So, a few months of more bullshit, I bought a big, fake ass ring." I wiggle my fingers, spinning the diamond, because the cheap piece of jewelry doesn't even fit right. "I led everyone I worked with to believe I was engaged to the love of my life. Two years later, I quit and moved away."

"You lied to everyone that whole time?"

"Yes." Why do I feel ashamed about it now?

Cole stares at me with his jaw clenching. The fiery frenzy we were just in somehow turns ice cold. I'm really rethinking what I've done and not for the first time...

"I can't believe this is goodbye day." My roommate, Jenna, skulks over and hugs me from behind. "I'm gonna miss you so much, Hales."

"You're so dramatic."

"I know." We've graduated. It's time to move on. "Promise we're still going to meet at least once a year for a girl's trip?"

"Hells, yes!" I dump more of my things in a box once she lets go of me.

It's a lie. We're not going to see each other ever again. Maybe we'll text once in a while, but that'll fade fast. It's inevitable.

Trust me. I'm an expert on this.

I grew up moving from place to place, never having lasting relationships. I can't imagine what it's like to have a childhood friend you grow up with and grow old with. Hell, I can't even imagine what it's like to plant roots somewhere. Every person in my life is temporary.

A knock on our dorm door makes my heart lurch. Squeezing my eyes shut, I blow out a big breath and open the door with a huge smile plastered on my face. "Hey."

Cole looks exhausted. Almost as if he stayed up all night thinking about today, just like I did. "Got your fave." He holds out a paper cup, and the scents of cinnamon and cardamom waft into my nose. "Filthy, just how you like it."

In my opinion, a dirty chai has only one shot of

espresso. A filthy one has at least three. He buys them for me all the time.

"You're the best." I take a sip before setting it on the empty end table by my bare mattress. "I'm just about done packing."

Cole stuffs his hands in his jeans and looks around my empty dorm room. The grey hoodie he's wearing is his favorite. It's the one he wears the most. He calls it his "emotional support hoodie". It's ninety-five degrees outside and he's wearing that thing like he's freezing.

I've never had an emotional support anything to help me through my tough times. I rely on coldness to get me through.

I like my emotions the way I like my water — bottled with the lid on tight. But over the past year, Cole somehow unscrewed my top, which has turned me into a sloppy mess of feelings I can't handle.

What started as a fun night led to an amazing year, and now...

It's over.

We both knew this day would come, so why does it matter? To be pathetic and sentimental about it only infuriates me.

He pulls the hood away from his head. "What can I take down for you?"

"Those two boxes over there can go."

I'm not one for holding things. I was raised to pack fast and light my whole life. Everything I own fits into three boxes and one duffel. He stacks the two boxes and heads out.

My roommate props the door open for him, and

after he's gone, a breath shudders out of me. I can't hold myself together. Sitting on the edge of the bed, I bury my face in my hands and cry.

"Oh, sweetie." Jenna sits next to me. "Why don't you just tell him?"

I shake my head, unable to talk. My throat closes and eyeballs leak. This is so dumb. I knew better than to get attached.

"Why not?" Jenna whispers, rubbing my back. "He's crazy about you, girl. Poor guy looks like he's been hit by a fucking bus."

All the more reason to not make things any worse than they already are. "We knew this wasn't forever."

"Well, maybe that's how it started. But things change."

"And that's exactly what I don't want." Swiping my tears away, I blow all my sorrow out in one massive exhale and pull myself together. Crying won't fix shit. Neither will confessing my feelings for Cole. "He's going for his master's in London. I have an internship in Boston. We're going to be on opposite sides of the planet."

"So?"

"So?" I toss my hands up. "We both agreed that our careers matter most at this point in our lives. Being in a relationship won't work." There's so much more that I can't say, so I leave it at that.

Jenna scoffs. "You're really going to walk away from him?"

"Yes. I'm better off with a clean break. There's no sense in pretending what we have is going to go

anywhere beyond this campus."

It can't.

Cole walks in clearing his throat. I swear the temp in the room plummets. My hands turn clammy. I feel sick to my stomach. "What next?" he asks, but his tone is harsher.

I match it because it's easier than letting him see me crumble. "That one over there, and the lamp."

He scoops up the box of bedding and my crappy floor lamp, then heads out again.

Jenna frowns as she watches him leave. "You're making a mistake, babe."

"I'll be making a bigger one if I derail us." It's better this way. It's got to be. I refuse to be a distraction for him, and I can't let him be one for me. Our relationship worked great this year because it was easy. Life after college will be way harder.

I need to make something of myself before I try to make something for myself.

So yeah. This is goodbye.

Once Cole loads my truck up with all my shit, he's covered in sweat and has taken his hoodie off. His bronze skin glistens with sweat, and his abs contract every time he takes a breath.

I'm going to miss every inch of him. His hard body, big heart, loud laugh, bold personality, the way he looks at me, the way he smells.

Stop. I can't remind myself of all the wonderfulness I'm about to leave behind. My heart already feels shredded.

"Welp." I stuff my hands in the back pockets of my shorts. "Thanks for everything." I want to touch

him, hug him. Tell him how I feel.

"Yeah. Thanks for everything."

We stare at each other for so long, I almost buckle under the pressure. A huge part of me wants to derail my entire plan and follow him instead. That can't happen.

My heart's racing a mile a minute. My hands won't stop shaking.

Heartbreak feels like a heart attack. I think I'm dying. Before I do something stupid like burst into tears and fall to my knees, I buck the fuck up and get this over with.

"So long, Cole." With an awkward wave, I step away and climb into the driver's seat, cringing because he doesn't say a word back to me. Starting the engine, I see Cole stare at me in the rearview mirror. Ignoring the pain in my chest, I drive off.

Shit, I can barely see the road with how blurry my vision becomes.

Fuck these emotions. Fuck these tears.

I leave without looking back, because if I see Cole for even one fraction of a second longer, I'll blow our futures up.

"If it's meant to be, it'll be." Glancing left, then right, before I make my turn on the main road, something in my passenger seat catches my attention.

Cole's hoodie.

With a shaky hand, I pick it up and smell it.

My heart collapses…

"How long do you plan to stay?" Cole asks cautiously. The sexy basketball player in a hoodie and jeans is long gone. This new man is different. More rigid. I like the easy-going Cole much more than this one. Maybe he has his guard up and that's why he looks so severe. I can't blame him.

Or maybe he's changed over the years, and this is who he is now.

Instead of saying what I want, I go with, "I'm staying for as long as I can."

He takes another step back from me, nodding as he stares at the floor. He seems to contemplate what his next words should be, and since I'm too fucking scared to hear them, I jump in and change the topic. "What do you think of walls? Can they come down?"

After a measured pause, he takes the bait. "Yeah. It shouldn't be a problem. I'll get some measurements and we can work through the details later." He shoves his hands in his pockets and walks away from me, going further into my new office space. "This is going to cost a pretty penny to build how you want it."

"I know."

"It's going to take time, too." His warning is clear. I'll have to stick around if I want this.

"That's fine. I'll work from home and hire staff in a couple of months. Right now, I'm focusing on networking and getting my foot in the door with all the right people. I'd like to hit the ground running once I have this space up and in good shape."

He swallows hard, his Adam's apple

bouncing. "How booked are you already?"

"Well..." I hate to admit this. "Not very. I've missed the window for holiday parties and weddings. Those would have been booked out months ago. I haven't had a chance to advertise heavily yet, because all my savings is going into this place." I run my hand along the dingy wall. "But my website's all good and I've got a ton of appointments set up to introduce myself to bridal shops, florists, and all that jazz. Hopefully, I'll hit spring wedding season with a bang."

"Solid plan."

"I have a lot of goals to reach."

"Some things don't change."

Is that a compliment or an insult? Before I can find out, Cole walks away.

Chapter 5

Cole

I'm fucked.

Haley and I kept things professional between us for the rest of the site visit, which gave me a chance to build my walls up. Being back in Haley's orbit is terrifying. It's crazy how she can turn her feelings on and off so fast. Her lust, too. I once loved that about her because we could fuck around all over campus, and she'd act like I hadn't just bent her in half and railed her in the laundry room fifteen minutes before ethics class.

Now I hate it.

I'm not good at shoving my emotions into a box. I feel everything and it all shows in my expressions, my voice, my body language. I'm a positive, upbeat guy, so it's usually not a problem. But when I hurt? Fuuuuck, I can't hide it at all.

The one time I tried nearly killed me. It was the day Haley left college. The day I heard her say, *"I'm better off with a clean break. There's no sense in pretending what we have is going to go anywhere beyond this campus."*

Sometimes I trick myself into thinking she was right that day. Everything we had was pretend. Yeah, people knew we were hooking up, but that's all we did. And studied together. Ate together. Slept together. Watched movies and partied together. Confided in each other.

She became my best friend. The love of my life. The woman I thought was my endgame. But we never put a label on what we were, and I never told her how I really felt. Haley wasn't in college to find a man, and honestly, I wasn't ready to wife up.

Our situation was perfect for us, and it all started with a game of flip cup at the beginning of junior year...

"Ohhh Mr. Hotshot thinks he can take on this?" Haley drags her hand down her body. Her tits spill out of her tank top while the beer sloshes out of her cup. "You don't stand a chance, buddy."

"Shots fired!" my boy Jared yells. "Get him, girl!"

Leaning across the table, I flash a huge flirtatious smile. "Baby, these fingers are fucking magic."

Haley's head tips back as she laughs. Standing on the opposite side of the table, she makes me want to climb right over it to kiss her. She's sexy as hell. We share a few classes together and it's hard to not get distracted by her. She wears this perfume that makes my dick immediately hard every time she walks by me.

"Game. On. Buster."

"Cole?" Jared cocks his brow. "You down for a one-v-one with this spicy girl?"

I drag my gaze down her body, making it very obvious that I like that idea. "Definitely."

"What's the winner get?" Haley asks, while Jared pours beer into the lineup of solo cups.

"Whatever they want from the loser."

She flashes me a sexy smile. "Perfect."

Jared rubs his hands together and gets the crowd pumped up. "Ready. Set. Go!"

I beat Haley before she's able to flip her second cup. Cheers roar in my ears as I saunter over with a big told-you-so smile. "Accept defeat?"

"Never." She keeps trying to flip the cup and failing. There are three more beer-filled cups waiting for her to flip after this one. She didn't stand a chance against me.

I flirtatiously bump her out of the way with my hip and flip it on the first try. Then she downs the next cup and I flip it for her. And we work in tandem until she's drained the cups and I've flipped them all over.

"Damnit." She laughs, her cheeks bright red. "You're too good at this."

I cock my brow at her and lean into her face. "Accept defeat now?"

A sinful smile spreads across her perfect mouth. "This doesn't feel like defeat to me."

Well, it definitely feels like a win for me. Especially with how she's pressing against my body, her cold little hands snaking around my neck. "I told you my fingers were magic."

"Guys say that all the time. They're always

41

wrong."

My dick hardens. "I don't lie. If I say I can do something, I can fucking do it."

Haley playfully walks her fingers across my chest. "What do you want as a victory prize?"

A lot.

Pursing my lips, I pretend like I'm debating, even though I've had my answer all along. "Answers to the Econ assignment due Tuesday."

Haley gawks at me. "How about a kiss instead?"

I shake my head. If I kiss her, I won't stop. "Econ answers."

Haley is one of the smartest in our class. I'm sure she's got that assignment done and dusted.

"I don't have them." She giggles. "It's not due for like another three days. I haven't even cracked the book open yet. Sorry about your luck."

I lean in and kiss her anyway. When we pull back, I lick my lips, savoring her taste. "Meet me at my place tomorrow at four. We can work on it together."

"Okay," she says, a little breathy. "Are you going to show me how magical those fingers are again?"

Dragging my gaze down her sweet body, I love everything I see. "Maybe, if you're a good girl."

Tuesday comes and while flirting our asses off with each other, we work for hours on our assignment, order pizza, fall asleep, and become inseparable from that day forward. We spend every spare minute together. I think I'm addicted to her.

I haven't tried to kiss her again, for that very reason. I swear if I do, I'll never stop. Haley's a drug *that, once she gets into my system, I'll never get out. It's already hard to keep things chill between us. I want to touch her. Fuck her. Keep her.*

Who wouldn't? She's fun, loud, crazy smart, ambitious, and carefree. She's perfection.

One night, just after finals, we leave a party early and stumble back to her place.

"Damn." Haley groans. Jenna tied a bandana to the doorknob.

"My place?"

"Let's go." She holds my hand while we make the long trek back to my house. It's off campus in a row of rentals the college keeps. "It sucks when everyone else is always having bedroom fun."

"Tell me about it." I live in a house with five other basketball players. We've got a revolving door of girls and the walls are thin. "So whatcha saving yourself for? Is it a religious thing?"

"Hell no." She itches her nose. "I just haven't found someone to play with yet. And I want to play a lot. Like all kinds of a lot."

What the hell does that even mean? "Like with sex toys?"

"Nooo." She stumbles into me, forcing us both off the sidewalk. I guide her back on track and hold on to her, so she doesn't trip and fall. "I mean yes, toys, but also cuffs and paddles and stuff. I wanna get spanked and called a good girl and be a dirty slut for your cock." She stops, her mouth dropping. "I mean, not your cock. But like, someone's cock."

Damn, that's cold. "Why can't it be mine?"

She slow blinks at me like it's preposterous to

think I'd have a chance. "You want it to be yours?"

More than anything. *"Well not if you don't want it to be mine."* Smooth, Cole. Real smooth. *"But aren't you going off the deep end, Little Miss V-Card?"*

"Meh." She tosses her hands up. "Go big or get off the porch."

"That is not how that saying goes." Bless her. It's go big or go home. And also, if you can't play with the big dogs, stay on the porch. I'm not about to correct her though. It's cuter how she said it.

Haley bats her lashes at me. "You want me to be a slut for your cock, Daddy Cole?"

I guide her up to my front door because I'm worried she'll fall. "You're drunk, girl."

"Be that as it may..." She spins around and slams her ass against the door before I can open it. "Do you want it? Me? Do you want me?"

More than my next fucking breath. *It's been hell pretending I'm cool with just being her party friend and study partner. "I want you sober before we have this conversation."*

"Mmmkay. I'll make pancakes in the morning, and we'll iron the wrinkles from the details."

Jesus, she's a mess.

I get her inside, tuck her in my bed, kiss her forehead, and leave an uncapped bottle of water for her, just in case. And a trash can. "Sweet dreams, Angel."

I crash on the couch. She'll likely forget this entire conversation by morning, right? She's pretty sloshed.

But what if she doesn't?

Do I tell her I'm a virgin too? Does that make me sound like a loser? Shit, what if she thinks I'm a liar? Maybe I can pretend this conversation never happened. I won't bring it up unless she does first.

She probably won't remember any of this.

The next morning, Haley wakes me up by straddling my hips, pressing my morning wood down with her pussy. She's in my favorite grey hoodie and no pants. Her bedhead's adorable. Her mascara's all smeared, and eyes are puffy with sleep. "Good morning."

I yawn so big, my jaw pops. "How you feeling?"

"You tell me." She grinds against my length, making me groan. I grip her hips to stop her. Thank fuck she's got panties on and I'm fully clothed. "I meant what I said last night." She leans down and presses a soft, minty fresh kiss to my lips. "I want you to be my first, Cole."

She didn't say those words last night. And now that she's sober, the weight of her confession feels even heavier. My heart pounds against my sternum. "You sure about this?"

Haley nods, biting her bottom lip. "You're the only one I want. I'm tired of pretending otherwise. I can't stop thinking about you. Fantasizing about you."

Holy. Fucking. Fuuuuuck.

Same.

Before I second-guess this whole ass thing, I lift Haley up and she wraps her legs around my waist. I carry her to my room, taking the stairs two at a time. "Give me a second," I say, laying her gently on my bed. Then I go into the bathroom, shut the door, freshen up, *and hunt down a condom…*

She hadn't been kidding about all the things she wanted to try, either. My girl made a bucket list that took us our entire senior year to check off. We even went to classes so we could learn Shibari, and I went down a rabbit hole to learn a bunch of other kinky things like how to play safely with hot wax and electroshock toys.

It was the best year of my life.

Until she walked away, just like she warned she would.

Haley always said she never had roots and didn't know how to make any. I came from a big family and my parents still live in the house they raised me and my four brothers in. Her home life was shit. Mine was fantastic. Neither one of us had been in a serious relationship before. I didn't have time for one. She said she never had the desire or opportunity because her family moved around too often.

It was never supposed to get real.

I was the dipshit who blurred the line between lust and love. Real and fantasy. Pretend and permanent.

She warned me over and over that she had big plans for her future. I said I did too. I still needed my master's, and she was offered a killer internship in Boston.

Haley didn't abandon me. She stayed true to her word. She kept her compass pointed north and never wandered off her path. I can't be mad about it. I should be grateful. Her making a clean break forced me to double down on my studies and finish my master's program in record time. I've got a damn good job now and have made a name for myself.

If she'd stayed, I would have asked her to marry me. I would have cut my education short and gotten a job at a smaller firm, which would have been fine.

But I wouldn't be who I am today. I know it.

When she drove off with my heart and hoodie that day, I told myself if we were meant to be, we'd be.

Love requires good timing. We didn't have it before, but maybe we've got it now.

Taking the elevator back up to my office, I wonder what the best-case outcome is now that Haley's crashing back into my life. I'm at a loss. She's already moved at least twice in the five years we've been apart. I'd be an idiot to think she'll stay in Banner Bay for any decent length of time, even if she's leased an office space and plans to renovate. I just don't think she has it in her.

And if that's the case, why am I allowing myself to have hope? Why am I staring at the number she saved in my cell? Why am I pulling up a text box? Why am I—

"Cole, come into my office," Noah orders, storming past me. Christ, I was in such a fog, I didn't even realize I'd made it up to my floor already.

My stomach churns. Noah's been acting weird lately, grumpy one minute, laughing the next. His polarizing shifts give me whiplash. It also feeds my inner fear of having the rug pulled out from under me.

I close the door and sit down. Noah's office is three times the size of everyone else's, and it has drywall instead of glass walls. The shades facing the main office area stay drawn and the afternoon light casts a golden glow on all his mounted plaques and awards.

"I need you to plan this holiday party. I'm too swamped."

"What? Woah. No, I don't know the first thing about..." *Timing. Is. Everything.* Sitting down across from his desk, a great idea hits me. "Okay. No problem."

Noah's brows fly to his receding hairline. "That was easier than I thought it would be."

"I'll do it on one condition."

"Name it."

"I get to hire someone to help me."

"Get Tamara to do it. I already pay her."

"Nah. I want a professional planner."

Noah frowns. "How much is this going to cost?"

"A lot." I'll make sure of it. "But you have to spend it to make it, right? This is for our biggest clients who have new properties popping up all over the country. Let's remind them how great we are and show how much we appreciate them."

Noah's bloodshot eyes widen, and his frown turns upside down. "Yeah. Okay. Let's make it big."

"Go big or get off the porch, you know what I mean?"

"No." He shakes his head. "Are you high or something?"

Laughing, I stand up and straighten my suit jacket. "Don't worry about the party. I've got it covered."

"Good." Noah clicks away on his keyboard, getting back to business while I head for the door. "And Cole?"

I look over my shoulder at him. "Yeah?"

"You've got lipstick all over your mouth."

Well, shit.

He arches his eyebrow. "That must have been a damned good site visit you were on."

I leave without saying another word and pull Haley's number up on my cell.

Cole: Want to help me plan a company holiday party?

Chapter 6

Haley

I stare at Cole's text message, my heart pounding in my chest. Holy crap. Is he serious?

Haley: Absolutely!

Excitement bubbles out of me. And before I read into why he's asking, I get busy with the basics.

Haley: What's the budget? Do you have a theme in mind?

Haley: Is this in-house or do you want to rent a space? Hotel? Museum? Art gallery?

Haley: Date?

Haley: How many people?

Haley: Cocktails and light food or full menu?

I've got a great concept in mind already if he wants a Winter Wonderland scheme. Or does he want something more festive, like candy canes and shit? Ohhhh, maybe they want a more rustic vibe with evergreens and holly? Hey, they might like jewel tones and funky décor.

Typing another question, I pause and look at what I've sent so far. Shoot, I need to back off a bit. He probably thinks I've lost my mind. He hasn't answered a single one of my texts yet and is likely already scratching his eyeballs out with frustration that I'm blowing his phone up.

Cole never was one for snaps and texts. He hates being on his cell.

My phone vibrates.

Cole: I'll get back to you.

He doesn't say anything else. The highs I felt twenty seconds ago crash to the ground. It's fine. All good. He probably wasn't expecting so much from me so soon.

That's a current theme for the two of us, I guess.

Sitting back on my couch, I put my feet up and blow out an exasperated breath. "Way to bombard him, Hales. You suck."

Running my finger over my bottom lip, my mind flashes back to that dynamite kiss we had earlier. Talk about mind-blowing. He's *definitely* changed.

Cole's a lot more aggressive than he used to be.

Does that go for all sex acts or just what he does with his mouth? My pussy clenches when I imagine him going to town down there.

Pulling up his Insta, I lock onto a photo of him playing basketball. He's dunking — arms up with the ball ready to slam into the bucket. He's so high off the ground, he looks like he's flying. It's my favorite photo of all the ones he's posted this year. I know I belong in the stalker category, but I don't care.

I've missed him every day and these photos make me happy. Every time he posts a new reel or photo dump, my heart cheers. Then it sobs because I've lost out on so much with this man.

It's my fault. No sense in crying over it anymore.

Scrolling through several posts, I stop on a pic of him fishing on a boat. Wearing sunglasses, a backwards baseball hat, and no shirt, his skin gleams with a sheen of sweat and I can count all six of his abs.

He's holding a beer in one hand and flipping the camera off with the other. He's got a huge classic Cole smile on his face that makes my heart melt. In the next photo, he's leaning against the side of the boat, looking to his right. The one after that, he's holding a huge fish. The one after that is of him swimming in the ocean—the water so blue, it's got to be in the Caribbean.

Returning to the first pic, I run my hand down to the joining of my thighs. I changed out of my pencil skirt and blouse the instant I got home, which means reaching my pussy is a whole lot easier in these sweatpants and hoodie.

Yes, I still have his hoodie. I wear it so often, it's a miracle the threads haven't disintegrated.

Shoving a finger in my pussy, I pleasure myself with the memory of how Cole kissed me earlier. It was wild, aggressive, possessive. As if the instant he confirmed I was single, he claimed me.

Dramatic and inaccurate, I know, but the thought makes me so horny I could die. I'm good at pretending. I've fantasized about this man ever since we played our first game of flip cup and I've never stopped.

I pretend he's here with me now, watching me get off.

"Such a slut for my cock, aren't you, Haley?"

"Yes, Daddy."

"You want that pretty little cunt filled, Angel?"

"More than anything."

"Earn it."

I will. I promise. Until then, I work my clit until my thighs shake and the release that's built in me all day long rushes out of me. The orgasm is decent, but, just like all the other times I chase a release by myself, it's nothing compared to what it used to be.

Clearly, I'm broken.

After washing up in the bathroom and getting ready to settle in for the night, I plop back down on my couch. A number I don't recognize lights up my cell. "Next Level Events. This is Haley."

"Hi, my name's Courtney, I um, got your number from Jenna."

I sit up and go into business mode. "Hi, Courtney. What can I do for you?"

"I'm getting married!" she squeals.

"Congratulations." I'll never tire of being happy for others. It's always exciting when someone starts a new chapter of their life. "Have you set a date yet?"

"June twenty-seventh."

"Wonderful. And where do you plan to have it?"

"I'm not sure yet. I was kind of hoping you could help me find a place. Actually, I was hoping you could plan the whole thing. I'm crap at making decisions and I'm too overwhelmed with even picking a theme. I thought I knew what I wanted my wedding to be like, but now that it's for real, I don't like anything I've come up with."

"No problem." I hop up and grab a pad of paper and pen from my big bag. "Tell me what you want and let me work my magic for you. Do you have a budget set?" She says there's no price too high for the wedding of her dreams and gives me a long list of things she thinks she wants, but says she's open to other options. It's a massive wedding with five-hundred guests on the list.

"I'd love a horse-drawn carriage, but that's not a deal breaker or anything."

"Okay." I furiously jot all her wishes down. "Do you have a location?"

"Somewhere in the mountains."

Somewhere. In. The. Mountains. That's not very specific. "Anywhere in particular?"

"I think Montana," Courtney chirps. "I want big green open fields with the mountains in the back. And enough flowers to be seen from space. Oh, maybe Colorado would be good."

Oh boy. "I'll work on a couple options and send a contract over for you to review and sign, then we can go from there."

"Perfect." She sighs with relief. "I already feel the stress lifting from my shoulders."

Yeah. And now it's on me. Normally, I love working with brides, but this one may be more than I can handle. She's all over the place with her wish list and if I give her what she's asking for, it'll cost a fortune.

I bet she'll bail when she sees the prices.

"How do you know Jenna?" she asks.

"We were roommates in college."

"Aww, that's cool. She's my cousin."

Great. Now I feel obligated to give this girl what she wants, even if I don't get paid for it. "Jenna's amazing."

"Yeah. She's nutty, but we love her."

"Well, if you think of anything else, just shoot me a text, okay?" I hate talking on the phone. "I'll work my magic and have some options for you in a couple of weeks."

"Wonderful. Thanks, Haley." She hangs up.

I have no clue if I should kiss or kill Jenna for this.

Haley: Your cousin just called me.

Jenna: You're welcome.

I roll my eyes and smile.

Haley: She's got champagne wishes. Does she have a beer budget?

Jenna: Hell no. Her fiancé is stupid rich. He

has more money than God.

That still doesn't ease my biggest worry. Courtney couldn't even decide a color scheme, aesthetic, or whether she wants it all outside. She just said, "I'll know it when I see it."

Those are the same people who tell servers to "surprise them" with a salad dressing because they can't decide for themselves. Ugh.

Haley: Thanks for the chance, babe.

I'll make it work. Bridezillas don't scare me, and I have plenty in my arsenal of ideas to work with. I'm sure we can put Courtney's dream wedding together in no time. And if she likes what I do, maybe she'll tell her friends about me.

Jenna: I got you, girl!

Jenna: Have you seen Cole yet?

I'm not sure I should say.

Haley: Yes. I met with him today.

My phone rings immediately, and Jenna's face pops up on the screen through FaceTime.

"Tell me *everything*."

I lean back with a sigh. "It was…" Awkward, scary, amazing, hot, weird. "Not as awful as I feared."

"Told you so." Jenna laughs. "He's still so hot, isn't he?"

"Hotter than hot."

Jenna kept up with Cole all this time. I used to get this horrible jealous feeling in my gut whenever I saw her like a post of his or make a comment, but it faded after she and I picked up our friendship again. It took Jenna a little over a year of texting me until I finally bit the bullet and continued our friendship. It wasn't hard, but it also wasn't easy. I had a lot to learn.

I'm so glad she was patient with me. I wouldn't be the same without her. In fact, I can't imagine my life without Jenna in it now. She's my best friend.

"Did he rail you against his desk or what?"

"No." I smack my head, laughing. "I wish though."

"What *did* he do?"

"Well, for starters, he took one look at me and dropped his coffee all over the floor. Later we met at the office so I could show him the space and tell him my vision."

"Ohhh, and how was that?"

"He brought me my favorite drink. Well, my old favorite drink."

"That chai stuff?"

"Mmm hmm." I sit forward. "And guess what? I'd brought him his favorite drink too." Come to think of it, I wonder if he really still likes double iced mochas or if he just took it to be polite, like I took his.

"What happened next? Did you two bang against the window and make up for lost time?"

"No, perv." I sit back with a sigh. "We kissed though."

"Woo!" Jenna yells. "Was it hot? Tell me it was hot."

"*Scorching.*"

"I fucking knew it! Cole's coming in clutch."

"Then we broke away and shit got super awkward again."

"Well, what do you expect, babe? He probably doesn't trust it."

I cringe. She's probably right. "I'm not giving up."

"Atta girl."

"He also just asked if I would plan his company's holiday party."

"Ohhh, that's a good sign."

"Is it?" I'm not sure.

"Fuck yeah! He's going to spend more time with you this way."

"No. There's nothing for him to do. I'll do it all. It's why I get hired."

"Make there be something for him to do, ya dumb bitch. God, Hales. You're so smart and yet soooo...."

"Talented."

"*Oblivious.*" Jenna tips her head. "Did he agree to design your office space, too?"

"Yes, but he was all business about it. Honestly, he went from blazing hot to freezing cold in a blink with me."

"How's it feel, babe?"

Ouch. "Horrible."

"Well, now you know how he felt when you—"

"I know!" I yell a little too loudly. Tears

burn my eyes and now I'm getting all sweaty. "I fucked up, Jenna."

"Isn't it great you're getting a chance to unfuck it up now?"

I don't feel good anymore. My stomach's in knots. "What if he doesn't want me back?"

"Then at least you'll have your answer."

Her statement reminds me of the kiss Cole and I shared earlier. *"Do you have your answer now, Angel?"*

"Anyways, have you watered your orchid today?"

"Yes," I say with a grin. "I put two ice cubes on her before I left the house this morning."

"Such a good girl."

Jenna gave me a purple orchid for my birthday three years ago. According to her, it's great practice at committing, without the burden of having to clean up after it. Orchids require patience, maintenance, and nurturing.

I suck at all three. At least I used to.

"She's got six blooms on her this time."

"Woo hoo!" Another phone rings in the background and Jenna gives me an *uh oh, I gotta get back to work* face. "Gotta run."

"Okay. Hey, thanks for sending Courtney my way."

"Anything for you, woman. You know I love you."

"Love you too."

We hang up, and impatience has me pulling

up Cole's text again.

Haley: Do you have dinner plans tonight?

I'm coming on too strong and I know it, but I can't bring myself to care. I feel frenzied and scared and I just need a little flicker of fucking hope here, damnit.

Cole: Yes. Sorry.

My stomach drops. There goes that.

I can't be upset about this. It isn't fair. I've been MIA for a long time and to drop into his life and expect things to go right back to how they were is so immature and stupid of me. I should be grateful he's seeing me at all. Part of me worried he was going to toss me out of his office this morning.

Haley: Np.

I set my phone on the coffee table and scrub my face. "Pull yourself together, Haley."

I need to move slower. Let things evolve naturally. I can't take this personally. He's got a life here. I'm a burden. I'm the problem.

Stop. Part of my *be-better* journey is recognizing when I'm getting toxic — with myself and others. Letting my past influence my present is not allowed. Yes, he has a life here. No, I'm not a burden. I'm not a problem for him, I'm a hopeful possibility. And if he doesn't want me, that's okay. I'm only partially here for him. I'm also here for myself, damnit.

My cell dings again.

Cole: How about tomorrow instead?

Chapter 7

Cole

I'll be honest. I have no clue what to expect out of this dinner with Haley, so I've come prepared for the best- and worst - case scenarios.

The Screaming Pelican is crammed with people at the bar. The restaurant side isn't much better, but I snag us a booth in the back.

Haley steps in, her cheeks rosy from the wind chill and she's all bundled up in a purple scarf and black puffy coat that hits her knees. She waves at me with this big, beautiful grin that makes me melt.

Jesus, how can I go back to feeling this way for her?

Easy. I never *stopped* feeling this way for her.

Standing up, I give her a hug before she strips out of her coat and says, "This place looks so fun!"

I ease back into my seat across from her. When she scoots into her side of the booth, her boobs bounce. My girl's got phenomenal tits. They're huge, heavy, and so fun to fuck. I remember them well.

She catches me staring and spares me the call out. "What's good here?"

I chose this place because it's not too romantic, and not too dive bar-ish. It's also my comfort zone. "Their brick oven flatbreads are decent. The gyros are massive. My favorite is the crab imperial stuffed chicken breast."

"Wow." She gawks at the menu. "They really do have a bit of everything here, huh?" Her brows knit as she studies both sides of the laminated menu.

"Welcome to the Screaming Pelican. Can I start you off with some drinks?" The waitress looks up and smiles. "Oh, hi, Cole."

"Hey, Mandy."

"You want a Modelo draft. Tall?"

"Yup."

"You got it." She looks expectantly at Haley. "And for you?"

"Um, I guess I'll have the…." Her gaze flicks over to the bar specialties and she frowns. "Root beer."

"Sure thing. You guys want any appetizers?"

I raise my eyebrows, letting Haley know she can decide for us.

"Loaded nachos, please."

As Mandy writes that down, I take a moment to appreciate how gorgeous Haley is. She also seems nervous, which is kind of cute. "Do you know what you want to order, Angel?"

Her old honorific makes her gaze lock on mine. "Umm. Yes?"

I tip my head at Mandy, signaling Haley to tell her what she wants.

"Can I have the buffalo chicken flatbread pizza. Blue cheese and carrots on the side. And a house salad with vinaigrette."

"Absolutely." Mandy turns to me next. "You want your usual?"

"As if you even have to ask."

Mandy sticks her pen back in her hair and walks away.

Haley and I stare at each other, and the restaurant noises become muffled. The auburn headed, hourglass figured bombshell from my past is all I see, hear, and want.

I've made a spreadsheet of all the clients we need to invite to this stupid holiday party, and I got all the answers to Haley's questions she sent through text. If this "date" turns into a business meeting, I'm prepared. If it morphs into something romantic, I'm also prepared.

"So…" Haley unfolds her napkin and places it on her lap. "Have you thought about what you want for your holiday party?"

Business it is.

"We have about fifty clients and twenty employees to invite."

"Spouses too?"

"Yeah, but no kids."

Haley digs through her huge bag, pulls out

a notebook, and jots things down. "Theme?"

"Don't care. Just not too Christmas-y or anything. Keep it neutral."

"Of course. Winter Wonderland with snow and ice, okay?"

"Yeah. That works." My boss won't even notice, anyway. He only cares about the bar and talking his head off to everyone.

"Budget?"

"Sky's the limit."

Mandy returns with our drinks. "Nachos will be out shortly."

"Thanks," Haley and I both say at the same time.

"And what about food and drinks? You want an open or cash bar?"

"Definitely open bar. I'm not sure about the food." We've never had a full dinner at one of these things in the past. It's always been crappy appetizers and little food stations. It might be a good opportunity to step things up a notch. "Let's do a dinner."

Her eyes crinkle when she smiles. "Okay."

"You got any places in mind?"

"Not yet." She clicks her pen. "But I will."

I love her confidence.

Our eyes lock and I lose my breath. If I'm not careful, I'm going to fall. Taking the upper-hand, I tilt my head to the side. "You got that look in your eyes, Angel."

She draws back. "What look?"

"The one that says I won't regret this."

The nachos arrive, but we don't tear our gazes from one another.

"I won't do anything you'll regret later, Cole. I promise."

She said that to me once before. Only then she was in a latex bodysuit and had me tied to her bed.

I didn't regret it for a second.

"What are you thinking about that has that goofy grin on your face?" She plucks a heaping stack of cheese-laden chips and puts them on her little plate.

"I'm thinking about that time you poured hot wax all over my chest and sucked me off."

Haley's chest rises and falls with her heavy breathing. Her next words are cautious as she sucks sour cream off her thumb. "Oh yeah?"

Grabbing a chip with three jalapenos stacked on top, I shove it into my mouth, hoping it'll stop me from running the damn thing.

My tongue sets on fire. Shit, that's spicy.

My eyes water and I grab my beer, chugging half of it.

Haley's still eyeing me like a hawk. "What was your favorite thing we did back then?"

"I don't have one." I loved them all. "What about you?"

She swallows hard before glancing away. "I think it was when you made me crawl to you on my knees, with that collar and leash around my neck." Her cheeks flush. "Remember that?"

Fuck yeah, I do. She'd lost a bet the week before and had to do my bidding for an entire day and night.

I'm still not sure what role I love more—being the Dom or the sub. Both work for me. But being a Dom worked best for me with Haley. It was the only time I had some semblance of control, and she was able to relax under my attention.

For someone who'd struggled to survive her whole life, being able to not worry was a nice change of pace for her.

And as someone who always goes with the flow, I loved being the one in charge.

Leaning back, I study Haley through hooded eyes. "You miss being on your knees for me?"

"Yes," she whispers, before plucking a chip off her plate.

Lust wars with anger inside me.

I want to punish her. I want her to grovel. I want her to tell me how she could leave and never contact me again. Because I know she kept up with Jenna. Jenna told me. I only have three friends I'm still in contact with from college—Jenna, Jared, and my old coach.

If Haley could keep up with Jenna, why couldn't she have done the same with me?

You're no better. You didn't even try to reach out to her.

Fuck that. I didn't do it because she didn't *want* it.

Anger wins.

"Am I supposed to pretend you didn't ghost me and leave a hole in my chest the day you drove away?" The words claw their way out of my mouth, leaving a terrible taste behind.

Our food arrives. "Let me know if I can get you guys anything else."

"Thanks, Mandy." I've lost my appetite.

I lean across the table and tap my finger against it. "Look at me, Haley."

She doesn't.

"So help me, Angel, if you don't fucking look at me I'll—"

"I'm not sorry for ghosting you, Cole." Her gaze lifts. "I'm sorry for taking so long to find my way back to you." Her hands shake as she lifts her glass and takes a sip of her soda. "I needed to leave everything behind. I wouldn't have done it if it wasn't absolutely necessary."

Words fail me.

"I had to work on myself. I was so toxic back then. And if I…" She carefully places her glass back down and folds her hands in her lap. "If I had any chance of deserving you, I needed to make sure I was worth it."

Why can't I find my tongue and use it right now?

"I had to work on myself, as well as make sure what I wanted was really right for me, before

I could work on us."

"Us?" The one word I manage to croak out feels foreign on my lips. "There was never an us."

She cringes. "Yes, there was."

"No, Haley, you wouldn't allow it."

Her chest looks like it caves in with her next exhale. "Cole, I—"

"I wanted to marry you. I loved you," I say, slamming my hand on the table. "And you knew it and still fucking left."

She shakes her head faster and faster. "I never knew any of that."

How could she not? "Bullshit."

She slams her hand on the table and our plates rattle. "You never once said you loved me, Cole."

She's right. I didn't. "That's because you would have left me even faster if I had and I couldn't risk it."

"And for that, I'm being punished now?"

"You don't know the first thing about punishment, Haley." I lean in, jabbing my finger on the table, punctuating my every point. "You didn't suffer like me. You didn't have to hold your tongue like me. You didn't have to stand there and watch the love of your life drive away like what we had meant nothing. You didn't lose weight because you sunk into such a depression, you couldn't eat or sleep for weeks. You didn't—"

"I can't do this." Haley shoves her notebook

into her bag.

"So much for sticking around," I snap at her while she packs up.

Haley glowers at me. "*How dare you.*"

"How dare I what? Look at you. You're packing up already."

"I was putting my notebook away, so I don't smack you in the face with it, you asshole!" Her whole face turns crimson. People start staring at us.

Holy shit, I had no clue there was this much resentment and anger still in me. Honestly, I feel like a jerk because I did this to myself. Haley's not the only one at fault.

"I'm sorry," she says, scooting out of the booth. She leaves her bag behind. With my heart in my lap, I watch her snake through the crowded bar area, holding my breath to see if she's going to walk out the motherfucking door.

She veers left to the women's restroom.

Relief surges through my veins. Shoving out of the booth, I bulldoze my way through the restaurant and straight into the bathroom.

"Cole!" she whisper-yells when I barge in. "You can't be in here."

"Fuck that." I lock the door so no one else can enter. "Look, I'm sorry."

"You have nothing to be sorry for. I deserve it."

The hell she does. "I had no right to be like that with you out there. I'm just confused and lashing out."

"You never said you loved me," she whispers. Bracing herself against the sink, she keeps her head down and back to me. "You never once said you loved me."

"If I had, would it have mattered?"

Her silence is answer enough. No. It wouldn't have.

"I needed to go." Her voice shakes. "There were things happening and I..." She shakes her head. "I couldn't let you be in my life anymore. Not until I could make things better."

I knew she had trouble with her parents, but that doesn't mean I couldn't have been there for her. "We could have taken on anything together, Haley." The fight's already left me. "Hey, look at me." Spinning her around slowly, I wipe her tears away with my thumbs and cradle her face. "We always made a great team, didn't we?"

She doesn't move. Doesn't speak.

"What happened back then that had the power to rip you away from me?" In college, I didn't think even an apocalypse could tear us apart. I've gone five years wondering what I did wrong. What made her run like I meant nothing to her at the end? "Don't say it was our careers and ambitions. We'd have made it work and you fucking know it."

She doesn't say a word.

Time to switch tactics.

"Angel." I run a hand through her hair and

tug it, forcing her gaze to meet mine. "What made you run?"

She stares up at me, and all the color drains from her face. "I got pregnant."

Chapter 8

Haley

I never wanted him to find out like this. Hell, I never wanted him to find out at all.

Cole tenses and this terrible, pained expression spreads across his face. "*What?*"

"I didn't want you to ever find out."

Wrong thing to say.

He stumbles back as if I shot him in the heart with a bazooka. His gaze flits all over the bathroom, most likely trying to find the fastest exit out of my life. "Are you for real, Haley?"

Tears I've held back for a long ass time, start flowing. "I didn't want to tell you because I didn't want you to be disappointed."

He stares at me with so much hurt in his eyes, I can't bear it. "Cole, I'm sorry." I try to come towards him, but he holds his hand up to stop me.

"Tell me everything. Right now. Right the fuck now, Haley." He sways. "I can't feel my legs." He squats down and buries his face in his hands.

"Cole." I reach out.

"Don't touch me."

I yank my hand back and kneel in front of him. "It happened so fast, I didn't have time to process it," I confess. "It was just before finals. I was two weeks late, and took a test. It came back positive. I went into a fog." My throat closes up. "I lost it three days after finding out. I didn't know how to tell you. Or even if I should tell you."

"Why would you keep something like that from me?" His voice cracks. "I could have been there for you, Hales."

"I didn't want to put that burden on you."

"*Burden*?" He drops his hands and stares at me. "It's not a burden to be there for someone you love. It's not a fucking *burden* to help when someone's hurting. It's not a *burden* to lose a baby, it's a fucking *tragedy*."

"One I tried to spare you from." I swipe my tears away and buck the fuck up. I've grieved over this a thousand times, and though this is the first Cole's hearing of it, there are more reasons for my actions back then. "I was terrified when I found out. You were so excited about UCL, and I had that internship in Boston. All our dreams were within our reach and the pregnancy would have derailed all of it. You would have given UCL up for me. For... us."

"Damn right I would have." His hands shake as he scrubs his face.

"I thought of a million ways to tell you. I just needed to get through finals first, and then I was going to say something so we could figure things out. But I lost it. To tell you after the fact made me..." I blow out a painful breath. "I didn't know how to handle it. I was all over the place with my emotions. It scared me."

"All the more reason you should have come to me about it." He reaches out and grabs my hand. "You should have told me."

"There was nothing that could be done by then. To tell you would have crushed you and I didn't want that either." Turns out, I spared him for nothing because he's still crushed. "I panicked. I went through a myriad of arguments in my mind, and they all landed on the same thing: I needed to cut ties with you before I dragged you down with me."

Cole drops back on his ass. "How can you think that? Why did you *always* think shit like that, Haley?"

My parents have always drilled into my head that I was a burden to them. They made me the scapegoat for every failure they had in their life. I was a financial burden, an emotional one, and a physical one.

"You know why, Cole." He's heard my childhood horror stories. In fact, he's the only one I ever told them to.

"It would have been different for us."

"Maybe," I admit, shaking my head. "But the chance vanished before we could find out." And I couldn't process the pregnancy fast enough, so I panicked and ran. "If I could go back, I'd do many things differently."

A breath shudders out of him. "Like what?"

"I'd have told you how I felt."

"Would you have still left?"

I'm not going to lie to him. "Knowing what I do now? Yes."

His shoulders drop. "Jesus."

"Only because I needed to work on myself, Cole," I rush to say. "I was so toxic back then. And maybe I still have a long way to go, I'm not even sure. But I had to break away from you so I could work on being a better person."

"That doesn't make sense. You're a great person, Haley."

"I was fucked in the head about a lot of shit." And he knows it, damnit. He just doesn't want to admit it. "I went to therapy for three years. I cut my parents out of my life completely. I've worked my ass off to be the best I can be so that…" I take a deep breath. "So that when I saw you again, you'd get the best version of me and could decide from there."

Without saying a word, he stands up and heads over to the sink to wash his hands in silence. He splashes cold water on his face in silence too.

Panic sinks its claws into my heart and starts squeezing. "Say something, Cole."

"I don't think words were meant for these situations." He blots his face dry and tosses the napkin in the trash. "I need time to process this."

"Okay," I whisper, taking that as my cue to leave.

But before I can unlock the door, he presses his hand against it to keep it closed. "Didn't say I needed to process it alone, Haley."

I close my eyes and let the tears fall.

● ● ●

Cole

Pulling her into my arms, I hug her tightly.

As mad as I want to be, I can't bring the emotion to life. Whether it was wrong for her to keep this secret from me or not is no longer relevant. She panicked and did what she thought was best. Haley thinks she's spared me the pain of something that was out of both our hands.

It kills me that she trusted me with so many of her painful secrets, but the one that involved *both* of us, she didn't share. I'm honestly confused about how to feel.

On one hand, she's right. The trajectory of my life would have been completely different if we'd had a baby. I fucking *love* kids. I want a ton of them one day. I would have given up my career in a heartbeat to have them with her. And part of me cringes because even though I'm not at all thankful she lost the baby, I am happy with how things turned out for me, personally.

Fuck me sideways. How selfish is that?

Yes, I would have given all this up if I had to. But I'm a little relieved that I *didn't* have to.

Talk about a clusterfuck. I'm a fucking asshole.

There's no doubt in my mind Haley would have been just as fast to put her life on hold too, and busted her ass to make sure my dreams came true at the expense of hers, if we could have that baby. She would have kissed her internship goodbye and settled for something less for us.

She's not a selfish person.

She's not vindictive either.

She was scared and didn't think she could lean on someone else because she's *never* leaned on anyone else before. I bet she was just as confused then as I am now.

How can I feel relief and failure at the same time about the same thing?

The bottom line is: We were young, and she found herself caught in a situation that scared the shit out of her. The universe made the choice for her so she wouldn't have to.

That little comment about not telling me back then because I would have been disappointed? That's her parents talking. I know it. Her parents couldn't afford their rent, let alone her college tuition. She'd busted her ass and got a full ride to college. Guess what her parents did?

Nothing.

No "good job" or "we're so proud of you."

They made her feel like shit and called her selfish for leaving them on the other side of the country.

I'll never forget the message I saw on her cell when she graduated. They didn't even show up for it, the fucking assholes. Instead, they sent her a text saying, "We hope you're proud of yourself."

To know she was battling the loss of a pregnancy on top of all that? Jesus fucking Christ, I want to scream.

Hayley likely thought I'd be disappointed that she'd miscarried. As if it was somehow her fault, which isn't true at all. She couldn't help what happened. I'd never want her to think that.

Or maybe she thought I'd be disappointed in her because I'd think she'd trapped me.

I wouldn't have. Not even a little.

Jesus, this is so messed up.

"Look at me," I growl against Haley's shoulder. "Turn around and look at me, Angel." She turns slowly until her back presses against the door I'm still holding closed. "Never again. Do you understand me? *Never. Again.*"

She doesn't budge.

"No more secrets. No more running. No more bottling up your fucking feelings. If we're going to do this, we've gotta trust each other, no matter what. And we're going to be there for each other, no matter what."

Her chin trembles. "I'm so sorry."

"Shhh." I cup her face and press my

forehead to hers. "You didn't do anything to be sorry for." She did the only thing she thought she could do. *The only thing she knew how to do.* "No more running, okay?"

"I'm not going anywhere," she says, hiccupping through her quiet sobs. "I promise." Haley grips my shirt and clings to me. "I've done so much work to get myself back to you."

I loved her when she was a mess. I've loved her all the years we've been apart. I love her now.

I can't help it. She's endgame for me.

"We're going to start with a clean slate." Resentment isn't a feeling I enjoy, and I don't hold grudges. I can't change the past, but I can protect our future. "You did what you thought you had to do back then. For better or worse, it's put us right here, right now. We just have to decide what we're going to do from this moment forward."

Haley stares at me, as if waiting for me to decide what that plan should be.

"We need to take things slow."

"Okay," she whispers.

"I'm not the same guy I used to be." She will not get her way just by batting her lashes or wiggling her ass.

"Neither am I."

"Take that fucking ring off your finger."

She slips it off and tosses it in the trash like a three-pointer. "Anything else?"

"Yeah." I lick my lips while staring at her for a heartbeat longer. "Kiss me."

She presses her mouth to mine, but it's nothing like what we shared yesterday in her office. This is painful. Slow. Tempered and cautious.

I can't stand it. Taking control, I show her how it's done.

When love gives you a second chance, you go all in.

Go big or get off the motherfucking porch.

Threading my fingers in her hair, I deepen our kiss and hold her flush against me. She makes a little moaning noise that sends blood straight to my cock. By the time I'm through kissing her, she can barely stand, which means I hold her up while she catches her breath. "You good?"

"Not hardly," she pants. "Jesus, where'd you learn to kiss like that?"

"I just told you." I back up so she can move. "I'm not the same man I was before. Take that as a warning." The playfulness in my voice still has an edge to it, so I hope she understands what I'm saying.

I could never fuck this woman out of my system, and lord knows I've tried. The upside is, I'm damned good at a lot of things now and she's about to experience all of it. The downside is, she might not be able to handle me anymore.

"Get back out to the booth. Our dinner's getting cold."

She nods, biting her lip and I slap her ass hard when she turns around to leave first.

"Get ready, Angel," I say against the shell of her ear. "Because by the time I'm through with you, you're not going to sit for a fucking week, let alone walk away from me ever again."

She looks over her shoulder and arches her brow at me. "Promise?"

Chapter 9

Haley

It's been a week since that dinner with Cole. We haven't seen each other since, but we've texted back and forth every day. He's been busy with work. I've been up to my nostrils making contacts around town.

"Welcome to the Metal Petal."

This is my fourth stop of the day. "Hi, is Tori here?"

"No, sorry, she's not in at the moment," says a young girl with bright blue hair. "Can I help you?"

"I absolutely *love* the pieces in the window. That blue and purple bouquet is giving big *I'll kill you while I kiss you* vibes." The navy-blue feathers look more like daggers poking out from the black dahlias. It's stunning. The arrangement next to it has black, red, and white flowers in an anatomical heart vase.

"Thanks. Those are from our Dark and Moody Collection." She beams proudly.

"I'm Haley." I hold my hand out for her to shake. "I run Next Level Events and am new in town."

"Well, we love working with other local business, especially women-owned ones."

"Same." I flash her a huge smile. "I'm actually planning a holiday party in mid-December." She pulls a face that makes me think they're already booked solid, but I keep talking and remain hopeful. "I don't need anything too extravagant. Just some small centerpieces for tabletops. And I can pick them up if I have to, no biggie."

The relief is plain as day on her face.

"I'm not picky about what flowers you use either," I add. "But I'd love it if the arrangements were edgy, like what you have on display over there. Minus the anatomical heart vases for this time around."

"That's not a problem at all."

Pro Tip: If you're easy to work with the first time, they're going to want to work with you again.

"I'm going with this kind of aesthetic." Pulling out my cell, I show her the inspirational photos I've saved for Cole's corporate party. It's going to be a showstopper.

I've hyper-focused on it all week because I want it perfect for him.

Sam pulls a pad of paper out from behind her desk and starts spouting out names of flowers and plants while she sketches a design. "Something like this work?"

My heart literally skips a beat when I see what she's drawn. "Perfect."

Ten minutes later, I've finished filling out the forms and have paid for the deposit. Easy peasy, lemon squeezy.

Sam holds her hand out again. "It was nice meeting you. I'll let Tori know you're the new party girl in town."

"Thanks. It was lovely meeting you, too. I can't wait to work with the Metal Petal again in the future." I hip bump the door and practically bounce out of there with a pep in my step.

I really like Banner Bay. I adapt wherever I move, but this place is quickly becoming one of my favorites. It's the first move that's all my decision too. Growing up, I was dragged wherever my parents drifted next. We were always getting evicted. I lived in a tent for six months when I was ten, and the back of a car for a few weeks when I was fourteen. To say my childhood was hard is an understatement. I didn't have friends. I didn't have choices. I didn't have shit.

The public library was always my safe space and there was one in every town I stayed in. Whenever I wasn't working or at school, I'd go to the library to read, study, nap. Stay warm.

I ended up going to the college that offered me a full ride. I'm just happy it was a great one, and it was clean across the states so my parents couldn't get to me. Meeting Cole there was a massive bonus. My internship in Boston was the only offer I had after graduation, and I took that too. My transfer to the New York office was strictly because I finally got a position that paid, thanks to the internship that didn't.

All my life I've made do, sucked it up, gone with the flow, taken shit, worked my ass off, starved, climbed, and penny pinched to make ends meet.

Moving to Banner Bay is a fresh start. I'm living it on my terms, and only mine. I've dumped everything I have into my business. I'd call it a gamble if I wasn't so confident in my skills. I'm damned good at my job and if I can show others that, then I'll never struggle financially again.

My cell goes off and joy lights me up like a fucking Christmas tree when I see it's Cole. "Hey."

"How's it going?"

"Oh, it's going." I smile, passing an older gentleman in a peacoat. "How's it going with you?"

I keep getting awkward when we talk, because part of my heart feels like no time has passed since college because of how easy we click. But the other part of my heart still holds its breath, feeling guilty for leaving him behind.

I bet he thought he didn't matter to me.

When the reality of it is, he means *everything* to me.

"I've got a surprise for you." Cole's voice is deep and playful. "Wanna see?"

His flirtatiousness trips me up because I'm still stuck in my guilty haze, while he's staying true to his word, and giving us a clean slate to work with.

I try my best to play along. "Tell me where to go and I'm there."

"My office."

He's working on a Saturday? That sucks. Then again, so am I. "I'm coming now."

His laugh spreads warmth down my spine. "I've heard those words before."

My cheeks heat. "I bet."

"How soon can you get here? I wanna be ready."

I still don't know my way around the bay area very well. "Probably twenty minutes? I'm over by the Metal Petal florist."

"Okay. See you soon."

"Do you want me to bring anything? Lunch? Coffee?" It's a little past three, but I haven't eaten yet, and maybe Cole hasn't either.

"Just that sweet ass, Angel."

Oh geez. He really wasn't kidding about starting fresh. The man's a menace to my heart and body.

After we hang up, I run in my high-heeled boots to get to my damn car faster. I haven't seen him since that dinner at the Screaming Pelican, and I miss him.

When I arrive at his office in twenty-five minutes, he's outside waiting for me. "Damn girl, do *not* run in those things. You'll break your ankles."

"I didn't want to keep you waiting." I slow down to a brisk walk until I reach him. "I hit every red light getting here. I'm so sorry. I didn't think you'd be waiting for me outside like this."

Cole's smile falls. Then he cups my face. "Stop apologizing, Haley."

My stomach knots.

"You don't have to rush to get to me. Ever. I'm a patient man, and you're worth the wait."

My heart twists.

He kisses my forehead, and the heat of his soft lips does little to thaw my frozen face. "Damn, you're ice cold. Let's get inside." He opens the door for me and once we're in the elevator, Cole gets this suspicious, playful smile on him. "Did you fall out of a vending machine, 'cause you be looking like a snack in that outfit."

I burst into laughter. "Dear God, is that how you pick up dates now, Cole?"

"Nah." The elevator door opens. "I pick them up like this." He scoops me into his arms and carries me out of the elevator while I squeal.

"I can't believe you're here on a Saturday."

"No rest for the wicked, I guess." He sets me down at the receptionist's desk. Dressed in jeans and a hoodie, Cole looks sexy as hell. I notice he's gotten a fresh haircut this week.

I'm not the snack here. He is.

Scratch that. Cole's a five-course meal.

And I'm *starving*.

"I've been busting my ass with some big projects this week and wanted to make sure yours got done as soon as possible." He holds my hand and guides me into his glass office. Without another word, he guides me over to his drafting table.

"Have a seat, Angel."

I'm too awestruck to obey. "Holy shit." My hands tremble when I touch the blueprint. Here it is. My office. My vision. "Cole, this is exactly what I wanted."

"Like I'd give you anything less?"

It's... *perfect*. I can't believe he's done this. And so fast too.

Cole gathers my hair in his hands and pulls it to the side to kiss my neck. I immediately feel dizzy.

"*Cole*," I groan.

"I've missed the way my name sounds in your mouth." He kisses my neck again, before slowly spinning me around to face him. Snaking his hand under my hair, he holds the base of my neck and locks gazes with me.

"I've missed everything about you," I confess. "You're my true north, Cole. I'm so sorry I—" My words cut off. He doesn't want me apologizing all the time, so I'll start practicing now. "I'm glad I found you."

He kneads the back of my skull and bites down on his bottom lip, dragging it across his teeth. "I'm glad you found me, too."

Don't leave me again, is what his eyes say, but his mouth stays shut.

Wrapping my arms around his neck, I kiss him slowly, sweetly. Except it doesn't stay that way. Especially when he groans into my mouth.

Our tiny ember of heat grows into a blazing inferno in a nanosecond.

His hands are all over me. We spin around his office, knocking things over, bumping into the glass walls. "Fuck," he grits out, lifting me up and carrying me to his desk. "You're killing me, girl."

"You seem pretty alive to me." I scrape his scalp as I bite down on his neck.

"Fuuuuck." He pushes away, his chest lifting with each breath he takes. "We gotta go slow, remember?"

Oh. Right. "Okay." I immediately shut down my lust as much as I can and hop off his desk. This kind of rejection is weird. Warranted, but weird. "I um…" How do I get out of this with any dignity? "I have a surprise for you, too."

He doesn't say a word.

"It's in my car, though. Let me just…" Licking my lips, I slip away from him..

He puts his hands on my waist, stopping me. "Stay."

Wow. Talk about confusing. This man is giving me mixed signals, left and right. That's not like him.

It's not like us.

We were never slow movers with each other. In fact, after our first time, we were on each other every chance we could get. A minute, an hour, a night, a weekend. Hell, he fucked me so good, I could barely get to class sometimes.

Maybe fighting that chemistry is what's tripping him up. I know it is for me. But Cole's right. We need to go slow. This isn't for fun. This is for keeps and we've got damage to undo.

He keeps his hands locked on my waist, his gaze burning into mine. I wish I knew what was running through his head.

"I'm not going anywhere," I whisper.

His intensity shifts a little.

Fisting his hoodie, I pull him closer to me so I can wrap my arms around him. When he hugs me back, I focus on the way his heart pounds in his chest. It's so fast. So strong. Not erratic like mine.

His cell goes off and he ignores it.

We just hold each other, leaving a million words left unsaid between us.

Which is our MO, right?

Fuck it. I refuse to let us repeat history when it comes to expressing our feelings. I'm not avoiding the hard stuff ever again. "What are you thinking right now, Cole?"

"You don't want to know."

"Try me."

His expression becomes guarded. "I'm thinking about all the time we wasted being apart. I'm thinking I should have hunted you down sooner. I'm thinking I should have gone with my fucking gut at graduation and asked you to marry me. I'm thinking I want to kill every man you've been with since then. I'm thinking I want to take you home and fuck your brains out. And I'm thinking that I really hope you *stay*."

"One." I hold up a finger. "We didn't waste time apart. We used it to get to where we need to be." I'll forever stand by that. I was not a good partner before, and I've busted my ass to become a better one since. Besides, Cole has a hella good job and seems happier than a clam with his life. "Two." I hold up another finger. "I'm glad you didn't hunt me down. I was the one who needed to come back when I thought I was worthy."

"Why do you always think your worth—" He stops and closes his eyes because it dawns on him why my self-worth is rocky. I was the kid who was told she meant nothing every day. "I hate your parents. I really, *really* hate your fucking parents."

"Oh look, one more thing we have in common." I hold up another finger. "Three, if you'd proposed to me after college, I can't say I'd have said yes, so that's a moot point. Don't pull the coulda, shoulda, wouldas with us. It'll drag you into a hole that I can tell you from personal experience is really hard to climb back out of."

He closes the space between us.

"Four, five, and six." I count with my fingers. "There hasn't been anyone since you. By all means, take me home. And trust me, I'm staying. There's no other place on the planet for me."

Cole stiffens.

Now that all that's off my chest and we're setting more things straight between us, I feel loads better. Leaning back on his desk, I smile. "This communication thing and talking out our feelings and worries is really working."

Cole keeps staring at me. "Repeat that, Angel."

"I said this communication thing is—"

"Not that. Number four."

I chew on my lip, recalling which point I'd made at four. Oh. Right. "There hasn't been anyone since you."

His chest collapses and he drops into his chair. "You fucking for real?"

"I would never lie about that." He knows it too. I've always been honest about my experiences, just not my feelings. "I haven't been with anyone else."

Something close to panic flies across his face. "Jesus." His head drops and he bends forward like he's going to be sick. "Haley."

"You're the one for me, Cole." I hop down to kneel between his legs so I can pry his hands away from his head. "There's only ever been, and only ever will be, *you*."

I'm sure he's been with other women. I left him and he moved on just like he should have. I can't be mad about it.

"I feel sick," he says, pushing away from me. "I think I'm having a heart attack." He clutches his chest.

Drama King.

I give him some space. "I didn't think my nonexistent sex life would be so damaging to your arteries."

He gawks at me. "You're really being serious right now? I'm the only man that's had you?"

"Well now you're making me feel pathetic." I turn around to march out. Playfully, obviously. "Let me go fuck a few guys right quick and I'll come back next week."

He grabs my hand and yanks me back, causing me to stumble into his hard chest. "You aren't going anywhere, Angel." His tone's dark. Register, deep. He slides his hand up my throat and cups my jaw. "There's no running anymore."

"It's about damn time we landed on the same page."

Chapter 10

Cole

After that confession she made in my office, I swear my brain can't operate. My dick, however, is functioning just fine. The instant Haley said she hadn't been with anyone since me, I devolved into a primal beast.

It's taking all my control to not mount her on the desk and fuck her senseless in my office.

But this fishbowl isn't secure, and I'll be damned if I risk us getting caught by security, a janitor, or one of the other employees who drag their asses in here on Saturdays like I do.

I know I said we should take it slow, but we've always been more like a bullet train. Why be anything other than what we naturally are together?

"Come home with me."

Haley beams with a killer grin. "Okay."

God, I love her.

How can I not?

There's so much about my girl that's changed, and yet, at her core, my favorite parts of Haley remain the same. After leading her back to my waterfront condo, I unlock the door and hold it open for her.

"Wow," she says, looking around my place. "It's very Cole in here."

I have no idea what that means. "Is that good or bad?"

"So, so good." She grips my hoodie and pulls me in for a kiss.

Annnnd our train goes from zero to a hundred and sixty in a blink again.

We pull at our clothing. Kick off our shoes. Scratch, caress, squeeze, and bite. We're two reckless animals in heat.

Once we're both stripped down to nothing, I carry her into my bedroom. Her wet pussy presses against my groin. Her legs are wrapped tightly around my middle. She smells divine.

"I've missed this," she groans as I lay her on the bed and slide down her body. When I lick her pussy, I love how she gasps. "Fuuuck, I've *really* missed this."

So have I.

Shoving two fingers into her, I flick her clit with my tongue and work my magic.

"Holy smokes." She arches off the bed. "What are you doing?"

See, there's the g-spot, then there's a deeper one that will make my woman beg for mercy. I'm gonna hit it until she screams my goddamn name.

"I want my name in your mouth," I growl against her tight cunt. "And I want my dick in it, too." I finger-fuck her so hard she claws the bedding. "You know the rule, Angel." I speed up. "Say it. *Fucking say it.*"

Her thighs shake as she pants. "You don't… get… until you give."

"That's a good girl." I double-down and flick her clit hard and fast with my tongue.

Her body clamps down on my fingers when she detonates, and the prettiest sound ever tears from her throat. It's my name she screams while her body grips and pulses around my fingers. I don't slow down. I'll drag the longest orgasm Haley's ever had in her life from her sweet body.

Then I do it again.

Every piece of her rattles apart as the second orgasm arrives almost as fast as the first. "Oh, my God!" Her body undulates and the second release flows through her like an immense wave.

When she tries to wiggle free from me, probably to catch her breath, I clamp my arms around her thighs and pin her down so I can lick every drop of her up. She tastes better than I remember. And she's put on some weight, which makes all her delicious curves that much more fun to worship.

"I'm blind," she says. "I seriously can't see."

"You gotta open your eyes."

When her baby blues land on me, her brow pinches. "Stars are dancing in my vision. You seriously just restructured my brain chemistry."

"I'm not even a little sorry." Leaning down,

I kiss her mouth before working my way back down her delectable body again.

"No, no, no." She smacks my head. "I need to recover before you go baaaaack!"

Too late. I've latched onto her clit again and there's no prying me off.

"Fuck, Cole. I can't come again."

She's wrong.

"You're going to be a good girl and give Daddy what he wants." I slip two fingers inside her, then work in a third, which makes her whimper. "Can you do that for me, Angel?"

Her eyes are hazy and heavy-lidded. "Yes."

And just like that, I've got her. She's putty in my hands.

Soon she'll be a puddle on my floor.

Dragging my tongue along her pussy, I alternate speeds and moves until I've tapped into the pleasure points that make her cry out. "That's my good girl. Give it to me. I fucking need it, Angel." Her body rocks as I fingerbang her a little harder, hitting her g-spot this time. "Look at me when you come."

Haley's gaze flutters up at mine. Her eyes cross when she comes a third time.

"That's it. That's my good girl."

She grabs my throat while riding her release. "Kiss me."

Our mouths clash, tongues twirling around each other, and when I pull out my fingers, I don't break our kiss as I shove them into her mouth.

Her teeth graze my digits, and I distort her lips, pulling her bottom one down playfully. "Such a pretty little mouth."

"You should fuck it," Haley says, her cheeks flushed.

Licking my lips, I climb off the bed and back away. "Crawl to me, Angel."

Haley slips off the bed and slinks over to me on her hands and knees. Her heavy tits sway, and her ass jiggles as she comes closer. For good measure, I back the fuck up and make her work for it.

"Show me how much you missed me." I thread my fingers through her hair and guide her mouth to my cock. She can barely get half of it in before she's gagging. "I love the sound you make when you choke on me."

Haley makes an undignified noise and her nostrils flare. Then she breathes through her nose and tries to deep throat me. Her eyes bulge when she gags again. Drool drips out of her mouth and down her chin.

"Wrap your hand around the base," I order, then drive my dick in and out of her mouth, face-fucking her. "God *dayem*," I groan. "You feel so fucking good, Angel." She slurps and sucks harder; the filthy noises crank my lust up ten more notches. "You drive me crazy." I'm reduced to grunts and pants while she sucks me off harder. Faster. "That's it. Keep going. You're sucking me so well." My legs lock. "More.

Mmmph. I'm close." She jerks my base while I fuck her mouth harder. "Keep going, good girl." Shhhhit, I'm gonna blow. Gripping her hair tighter, I growl, "*Swallow.*"

My cock throbs as the orgasm rips out of me and shoots down her throat. I grunt and groan like a mindless animal until I'm spent. One step back and my cock falls out of her mouth. It swings heavily between my legs as I bend down and grab Haley's arms, lifting her to her feet. We kiss like it's the only way we can draw air into our lungs or get our hearts to beat. As if our entire existence is to be tangled up in each other.

I can't explain this unimaginable, potent, heady connection we've had since day one.

"I feel like I've loved you in all my lifetimes," I say against her mouth.

Running my hands all over her body, I kiss down her throat and suck one of her big nipples into my mouth and pinch the other. She hisses through clenched teeth and holds steady for me. "I don't remember you being so rough. I like it."

Good. "Then you're really going to like what I do next."

Chapter 11

Haley

I'd live my whole wretched life all over again if Cole's the prize at the finish line. Everything in here smells like him. The hoodie I've kept all these years lost his scent long ago, and the couple of times I've been with him over the past week were in public spaces where fragrances mixed.

Here? In his condo? It's all him.

A million memories cyclone around me. All of them are so amazing they make my heart squeeze.

Cole carries me over to his bed again as if I weigh nothing. His arms are bigger now. His sexuality's intensified too. I hope I can handle his level of heat.

Holy shit, what the hell did he do with his fingers inside me earlier? Laughter bursts out of me.

"What's so funny, Angel?"

"I'm just thinking how you always bragged about your magic fingers." I wink. "Gotta say, your magic powers have leveled up."

"That's not all that's leveled up." He reaches under his bed to pull out a box. "Not to be presumptuous but I went ahead and got us some fun toys."

Oh my God. He went all out. But one thing in the box isn't new, and it's what makes me wet most.

I pull out the paddle that's got *Daddy's Angel* engraved in it. "You kept this?"

"Of course."

He says it like he knew I'd come back to him one day and we'd need it.

I dig through the box and pluck out a blindfold. I twirl it playfully around my finger and pull out a ball gag. "Is this for me or you?"

"Whoever wants it more."

I point out a stainless-steel butt plug. "What about that?"

"All you, Angel." Cole maneuvers me onto his lap and guides my head down to the mattress so I'm over his knee. "Cover your eyes for Daddy."

My heart leaps into my throat. Slipping the black satin blindfold on, I'm thrown back to the first time we did this. It was exciting and scary. Addictive.

Cole's big hand runs along my ass and my pussy clenches.

Thwack!

Pain radiates out from my butt cheek.

Thwack!

I can barely breathe.

"How's that feel?"

"G-g-good."

"Good what?" *Thwack*!

"Good, Daddy." The burn feels amazing, but the next hit makes me yip.

"My Angel's ass is redder than a cherry." He rubs his hand over my backside. "Just how I like it." He dips his hand between my thighs. "Fucking soaked." He shoves his finger in my pussy, twisting it until I moan. I have no clue what he's hitting in there, but it's phenomenal. "Spread your ass for me."

Precariously balanced on his lap, I reach back and do as he says.

"That's my good girl." He spits on my tight hole and circles his finger around it. I melt into his lap. "So fucking tight *everywhere*," he groans, sinking his finger in my ass. "What a needy little thing you are. No one's fucked these holes in so long."

I'm too stupefied to talk.

"You want Daddy to fill them, don't you?"

I nod.

Thwack! He spanks me with his hand and grabs my ass cheek hard, jiggling it. "Use your words."

"Y-yes." I swallow the saliva building in my mouth. "Please, Daddy."

Cole pulls out and lowers me onto the floor. "Stay on your knees." I hear him walk away and water runs in another room. Then I hear him go further away, like he's in the kitchen or something. I don't have a clue. I'll just wait here, blindfolded, like his good girl, until he comes back.

Footsteps sound behind me a few minutes later, but he doesn't touch me. There's a lot of rustling and plastic scrunching. Blood rushes to my ears because anticipation is pumping adrenaline through my system.

"Do you trust me?" he asks against my ear. His voice sounds a little muffled.

I think my hearing's getting wonky. "Yes."

"Will you let me collar you?"

My body melts more. "Absolutely."

"Can I fuck you?"

"If you don't, I'll scream." I'm desperate for him.

"Angel, you're going to scream no matter what."

My pussy clenches.

"What's off limits?"

"Nothing," I say. "You can do anything you want." I won't tell him no. I loved everything we used to do, and that hasn't changed. "Make me your fucktoy."

"Fuck, Angel. You have no idea what you're tempting me with."

Yes, I do. "If I can't handle you, I'll say mocha."

Something thick wraps around my neck and

then Cole's fastening the buckle. "Too tight?"

I swallow and move my head around. "No. It's good."

He hooks what I assume is a leash to me next. Then he slowly lifts the blindfold off my head.

Oh. My. God.

Cole's wearing a skull mask that covers his mouth, head, and neck, leaving only his eyes for me to see. He lifts it up just enough to show off his sharp jaw line and smiles. "Ready to play with me?"

Hells *yes*, I am.

Who is this man? I mean, me and Cole did fun shit before, but this is wayyyyy hotter.

He grabs the leash and tugs it. "Crawl."

I happily do as he orders. It's degrading and fun. Precious and sexy. It makes me feel super vulnerable and strange.

It also makes me feel powerful and confident.

Cole wants me. His hard dick says so. And the way he carefully moves around his bedroom, pulling my goddamn leash, I know he's testing the waters with me. "Such a good girl." I can hear the smile in his tone. "Maybe you needed a short leash all along. That way, you couldn't run from me back then."

He tugs, forcing me to stand. Then he slowly winds the leash around his hand to reel me in. "Would you like that, Angel? To be leashed for me?"

My mouth runs dry.

"You want me to come home to you every night, fuck your needy pussy until it's dripping with my cum, take every hole you have and make you beg for this cock?"

Yes. Yes. Double yes.

"You want me on my knees for you, Angel?" He drops down and tips his head back to look at me. I wish he didn't have the mask on so I could read his expression. But maybe it's easier for him to say this if he's hidden. "Want me to wreck your body every day and put you back together, piece by piece, just so I can fuck you apart again?"

I swallow hard.

He pulls the leash, tugging me down to him. "You're mine now."

Cole runs his hand between my tits and slaps one of them. I barely feel it. I'm so strung out on his words and the way we're acting with each other; I think he'll have to hit me harder to make it penetrate. I blindly reach for the paddle that I know is somewhere on the floor. My hand closes around the handle and I silently hand it over.

He tips his head to the side but doesn't say a fucking word.

"You want to own me?"

His gaze narrows.

"Then fuck me like you own me, Cole." I

shove the paddle into his chest. "And brand me, so neither of us forget who I belong to."

Every muscle I can see on him tenses and flexes. "Turn around."

Oh boy. This is going to hurt.

I can't wait.

Spinning around slowly, I push my ass out and look over my shoulder. "Spanking's the only way I learn, Daddy."

He's frozen in place, staring at me. Then I swear I hear him whisper, "Fuck," under his breath.

Satisfied with my delivery, I face forward and reach between my legs. "Spank me while I cum."

He might have me on the leash, but I'm the one in control. Rubbing my clit, I should be ashamed of how wet and swollen I am. My fingers are slippery from my arousal. I play with my clit, anticipating the first strike, getting more and more worked up about it.

Cole's hot hand is velvet on my ass as he rubs my cheeks.

Thwack!

The sudden sting makes me pitch forward.

"Again," I pant, rubbing my clit harder.

Thwack!

Holy shit, that feels so good.

"Again," I say, my voice cracking.

Thwack!

I see stars.

An orgasm builds and my lower half feels heavy with need. "Again. Please." I look over my shoulder at him. "*Please.*"

Cole could give Adonis a run for his money. The hard planes of his torso, the veins in his forearms, his sheer size—holy shit, when he finally fucks me, I'm going to blow apart.

He jerks the leash. "Turn around and face the wall."

"Yes, Daddy."

I brace for impact, counting the seconds as he makes me wait for my reward. But the paddle doesn't come down again. There's a muffled rustling noise, and the collar tightens around my throat as he uses both hands for something.

Then Cole nudges my legs apart and presses his cock at my entrance.

"Ready for me, Angel?"

I hope so. He's hung like a horse.

The first couple of inches stretch me out. He works his way in slowly, giving me time to adjust.

"That's it. You're doing so good for me." Cole runs his hand along my sore ass cheeks, pushing in and out of me a little at a time until he's fully seated. "Holy shit, you're so fucking tight, Haley."

I swallow hard. Saying my real name right now makes me feel more vulnerable than anything else we've done so far.

"Fuck me," I beg. If he doesn't start moving, I'm going to scream. "*Please* fuck me."

107

Cole pulls my leash, making me tip my head back. "You look so beautiful with my cock inside you, Angel."

A tear falls from the corner of my eye, and I honestly have no clue if it's because I'm overwhelmed, just right, breaking apart, or something else. All I know is, this feels so good I don't want it to ever stop.

"I fuck myself with memories of you every night," I confess. "Your touch, your voice, your smell, your hands on me... your dick inside me." He grips my ass and shoves into me harder, making me gasp. "This is so much better than that."

Our bodies slap together. He fucks me until I can't catch my breath. Sweat breaks out down my spine. My cheeks tingle. "Harder, Daddy."

Cole slams into me faster. Deeper. I almost can't take it.

A groan rumbles out of him, and I look over to our left at a floor-length mirror to watch us. The collar on my neck, the leash around his hand, the way he towers over me, how his muscles flex, the jiggle of my ass and thighs, the sway in my tits when I pitch forward and rock back. We're insanely hot together.

Cole rips his mask off and tips his head back, squeezing his eyes shut as he picks up the pace.

Watching him come undone in our reflection kicks me right over the edge. My pussy pulses around his cock and he lets out a roar that rattles my motherfucking bones. I feel every twitch of his big dick inside me. He holds my hips, shoving himself as deep as he can get. The pain is delicious.

Once he pulls out, Cole climbs to his feet and looks down at me. It's like everything we've just done catches up with me all at the same time. My pussy's sore. My ass burns. My knees hurt.

"I've got you." He gently picks me up. My leash drags on the floor behind us as Cole carries me into the bathroom and lowers me to my feet. "Can you stand?"

I nod. My brain's taking forever to catch up with the rest of me.

He unlatches the leash and unbuckles my collar. Cool air hits my neck, offering sweet relief. I didn't realize how tight it was before. It kept me secure while the rest of me kind of checked out.

Cole runs a hot shower and finally pulls his condom off, tossing it in the trash. "Come on, Angel." He ushers me inside the shower.

We're quiet for a while. I'm so exhausted, I can barely keep my eyes open.

Cole tips my chin. "You okay?"

"Yes."

"You sure?"

I'm suddenly exhausted. "That was amazing."

He grabs the soap and a fresh washcloth. "You don't mind how rough I was with you?" He gently scrubs my shoulders first.

"Not at all." I lean back against the wall and let him take care of me. "You definitely leveled up your dick game, buddy. Or my memories have weakened. I'm not even sure which. I swear you just fucked the last brain cell out of my head."

He laughs, rinsing me off. "Can I wash your hair for you?"

God, yes. "Please."

He dumps a ton of shampoo in his hand and massages my scalp. "Did you like being my fucktoy, Haley?"

"Yes." I stand up and let the water pour over my head while Cole rinses my hair out. "I really love the collar and leash."

"Good." He runs his hands down my body and twists my nipples. "Because you're going to be in them a lot more from now on."

Chapter 12

Cole

I knew ordering all that new shit online the other day was going to be a game changer. I just didn't think we'd be using any of it so soon. I'm not complaining. Might as well get my kinks all out on the table the first time I have her over, right?

Not gonna lie. I was a little scared she'd freak on me.

Yeah, we experimented with some of this stuff back in the day, but I wanted to get really damn good at being a Dom, for myself, and for my sub. In college, Haley opened a pandora's box inside me and when she left, she might have taken my heart with her, but she left me with all my desire and a penchant for punishments and rewards. Wearing a mask is heavy on my list of likes, too. It puts a barrier between me and my sub and gives me an opportunity to get out of my head.

Bonus points for the fucktoy fun.

Haley and I once spent two weeks with her as my fucktoy. She wore this little beaded bracelet on her wrist that was my permission to use her however I wanted. No questions asked. Nothing in return. I could take her in the laundry room, the football field, her bed, my house, the car, the janitor's closet. Wherever. I'd fuck her face, her tits, her ass, and pussy. I used her however I wanted and got off as many times as I physically could. Hell, I even crashed some of her classes and pulled her out of them just to sneak us into a closet so she could suck my dick.

And though the pleasure was supposed to be all mine with that bracelet back then, I will always stand by rule number one: If a man doesn't give, he sure as hell doesn't get. I made Haley come as many times as I could before chasing my own release.

I take care of what's mine.

When the bracelet came off, the game was over.

The collar I bought her is a much bigger version of that bracelet. I'm glad she enjoyed being leashed. She was fucking hot in it.

After we clean up in the shower, I dry her off first and take care of myself last. It's already dark out, and I'm suddenly exhausted.

"I should get going," Haley says, after redressing.

My stomach drops. I don't want her to go. "Stay."

She tucks her hair behind her ears. "I can't. I've got so much work to do, it's not even funny."

Then her eyes widen. "I forgot to show you!" She excitedly digs her phone out of her big bag and taps her finger on the screen. "I booked the Gantz Plaza for your party. It was a miracle that it was available. They asked if a Wednesday worked, I took it. You said it didn't matter what night it was on." She looks up at me. "I hope that's okay."

I clear my throat. "Yeah. I don't think it matters."

"Well, usually it would. People are busy and it's the holiday season. Weeknights are rough."

"Not as rough as weekends."

"That's what I was thinking." Haley holds her phone out. "Here's the theme I'm going with."

There's a bunch of white lights and trees and snowflakes and stuff. "Looks great." What else can I say? It looks like a big, white, elegant party.

"You don't like it." She takes her phone back, looking like she just got sucker-punched in the gut. "I... I can change it up. It's not too late. I'll cancel the orders I've placed and—"

"Whoa, whoa, whoa." I rub her arms. "I didn't mean it like that. What you have is amazing. And I know damn well you're going to put together a banging party for my company. It's just hard for me to envision it all. Even with the pictures."

Her shoulders drop and she tilts her head to

the side. "Cole, you literally walk into an empty room and can re-design the whole ass place and put it to paper."

"I can work with what people give me as their vision within the parameters of an existing building. I don't have the chops to design an entire blank space and turn it into a building."

"Bullshit," she snaps. "That's total fucking bullshit." Her eyes narrow and she shoves a finger in my face. "Who told you that? I'm gonna cut out their tongues."

God love her.

She's not far off the mark, either. "I've been busting my ass for three years at NGC and they never take my designs." I keep trying, but the rejection feels worse and worse with each submission. "The shit part is, when we have a new client, I get my hopes up that this will be my big break. Hell, I just submitted a design to put in a brand-new Marine Life Center, spent *months* working on the concept, and handed it to my boss for submission, even when I know I will not get it."

"Why do you think that?"

"Because I never do." Isn't she listening? "My ideas aren't what people want, I guess. They're not good enough."

Haley wraps her arms around my middle and hugs me. "Well, I'm proud of you for not giving up. And fuck anyone who doesn't like your concepts. They're stupid people with shit taste. You're more than good enough, Cole. You're too good. Too good for NGC, I know that much."

I appreciate the hype, but it doesn't matter. Constant rejection tells me where I stand on skill level. It is what it is.

"Promise me something?" She looks up at me. Damn, she's so beautiful. "Promise me you'll keep trying. Someone out there will appreciate your vision, Cole. You're such a talented architect." She playfully shrugs her shoulders. "I mean, I only hire the best to work with, and I hired *you* soooo, clearly, you're the greatest architect in the whole wide world. I'd settle for nothing less."

I'm not telling Haley I'm designing her office for free. She wouldn't like the handout. But she's not listed in our database, and I didn't have her sign a contract.

She's right. I just have to keep my head high and try harder to climb the ranks of success. I should be grateful I got the job I have, and I really love my work. I just wish more clients liked my concepts. They don't even give feedback on what they hate about them.

This past year was the hardest yet. Three potential builders all shot my designs down. Noah said to not take it personally, but that's easier said than done. Each time, someone else in the company got the job instead. I mean, hey, good for them, man. That's great. But it still hurts my pride. Their concepts were basic and lazy, in my opinion. If you're going to build something, make it fucking amazing.

I've been working with smaller clients this year, and also my brother Trey when he needs me, just so I can feel less of a failure. I guess my talents are in revamping existing floor plans, not erecting something out of nothing. One has my heart. The other has my soul.

"Your ideas for the company party look phenomenal," I say, bringing the focus back to her. "I can't wait to see it come to life."

Haley's expression softens. "Trust me. I'm going to blow this out of the park."

"Damn straight you will. I only hire the best."

"Touché." She drags me down for another kiss and blood rushes to my dick. Then her stomach growls. Loudly.

"Damn girl, you got a goblin in there or what?"

"Ugh, I've been running ragged all day. I kept meaning to stop and eat and never did."

Then she came home with me.

"What do you want?" I pull her into my kitchen and open the fridge. "I can make spaghetti, Alfredo, some lemony parmesan cream sauce?" Basically, all I have that's quick to make is pasta.

"No, it's fine. I really should get going."

It's not fine and I don't want her to go. "You

sure you can't stay for a little while longer? I can order food to be delivered, or we can go out someplace."

"Cole." She sighs. "I'm not running."

"I know."

Do I though?

I'm starting to think that's why I just got too clingy for my own fucking good. All this week we haven't seen each other, but her texts come through like little blips of hope, and part of me fears this is all just temporary and something will make her disappear again.

Shit. "I'm turning into a level five clinger, aren't I?"

"No." Haley giggles, tossing her hair and batting her lashes at me. "You're just obsessed with me."

She's not wrong. "Can you blame me?"

My girl's playfulness vanishes. "I get it," she says, softly. "It seems too good to be true. Us, I mean. We're too good to be true. For us to pick up instantly where we left off seems surreal."

I nod, my throat tightening.

Haley cautiously laces her fingers with mine. "Come home with me. I want to show you something."

Chapter 13

Haley

I don't think I realized how badly I hurt Cole, leaving him all those years ago. I was so scared and heartbroken back then, my survival instincts kicked in and I took off. The end. But seeing Cole's reaction when I said I had to leave his condo struck a chord. Even his comment about maybe he should have put a short leash on me all along so I couldn't run away really hits home. He said we should start over with a clean slate, but that can't happen. Too much still hangs in the air above us.

I'll do anything to prove my intentions to him and make us right.

If he asked me to marry him today, I'd say yes.

There's no other man for me. There never has been.

If we're going to give our relationship a second chance, I need to bare my soul.

We drove separately—Cole's idea, not mine. When he pulls into the parking spot next to mine, I compare us, just like I always used to do.

He has a black, sleek Mercedes. I've got a fifteen-year-old Subaru with a big dent in the front fender. I've never been one to give a shit about vehicles. If mine gets me from point A to point B safely, I'm happy. But as Cole climbs out of his car, he looks successful, powerful, and fine as hell. I probably look like a bum.

"How long ago did you move here?" he asks, walking over to me.

"About a month ago. It took me a while to find an affordable place in the area. Even longer for an apartment to open that I could snag. All my money is tied up in the office space, so no house for me yet."

He frowns. "You've dumped *all* your money into that office?"

"Into my future success, yes." I unlock the door and let us both into the building. "I saved enough to put a mean chunk down on construction and furniture, and signed a seven-year lease, which was the only way I could even get that damn property. Might as well make it exactly what I want the first time around instead of settling and making do with how it is for a few years."

He grabs my arm, stopping me mid-way up the stairs. But he doesn't say a word. His expression is filled with questions, though, and I can read him well enough to know what they are.

I guess it's easy to think my actions are out of character for me. "I meant what I said, Cole.

I'm not running anymore. I want roots."

And I want to plant them with him.

After opening the door to my not-too-shabby apartment, I shake off the urge to apologize for the messiness. Cole won't care if I have clothes and stuff everywhere. Since I've been working out of my house all month, there are folders, binders, and party supplies everywhere. Votive candles, glass vases, linens, and all kinds of shit I've collected on my own are stored in boxes stacked in the dining area I never eat in. If I can rent those things, I will, but if my client is on a tight budget, I use what I have so their parties are more budget friendly. I know what it's like to not be able to afford the things I'd like. It's become a mission of mine to give others the best events possible without breaking their bank accounts.

"I'm going to get into something a little more comfortable," I say, heading to my bedroom. "Make yourself at home."

"Okay."

It takes me less than two minutes to strip out of my stuffy clothes and into something way better. Keeping quiet, I cautiously watch Cole in my living room. I knew he'd snoop. It's why I wanted to bring him here. Cole's a curious guy who will ask a million questions until he knows everything about everything. He made it so easy to open up to him back in the day. It never felt like he was prying and being nosy. He genuinely liked knowing even the most insignificant things about me.

No matter how opposite we were, he'd find a way to relate to me. I did the same with him.

Cole casually walks over to my small bookshelf. Little notes are taped all over it. The one he's reading now says, "*You're not a hindrance just being in someone's life. You're a human, not baggage.*"

His jaw ticks. He swallows hard when he reads another one that says, "*No one can make you feel worthless without your consent.*" And next to that one is, "*Love yourself how you want others to love you.*"

My chest feels like it's cracking open only because I sort of feel like a weirdo having all these notes and sayings plastered in places. But I still have bad days when I need the reminder that I'm not trash.

Working on undoing the damage my parents did to me is an ongoing process.

He plucks a book off the shelf and fans through it. Colorful tabs stick out from the pages. I've written all over the margins of just about every book I own, marking things so I can reference them when I need to. His mouth moves as he reads, his finger running along the words. He slams the book shut and pulls out another, then another. "Jesus," he whispers.

"I told you I had to work on myself."

Startled, he drops the book on the floor.

"Shit." He picks it up hastily, but when he looks at me, he almost drops it again. "Is that…"

"Your emotional support hoodie?" I tug the hem which reaches my mid-thigh. "Yes. It's seen me through a lot."

Cole silently places the book back on the shelf, but his eyes remain fixed on me. "It's seen me through a lot, too." He closes the gap between us and runs his hand down my arm. "Was it always this small?"

"I think you've just grown." My heart skitters when he pulls the hood over my head, cocooning me like how he used to always wear it.

"I thought you would have tossed it out the window."

"Never." I exhale a shaky breath. "It's all I had left of you."

He tugs the hood back down and brushes the hair from my face. "Did it help?"

"I'm here, aren't I?"

His gaze drifts back to the bookshelf. "Yeah, you are."

"You know, you never even asked me about my pretend boyfriend."

His attention snaps back to me. A dark eyebrow lifts and he looks downright possessive. "You got a story for that fake motherfucker?"

"I never said he was fake. I said he was pretend."

Cole tilts his head. "There's a difference?"

"Absolutely."

He crosses his arms. "Okay then. Tell me about him."

Is Cole jealous right now? How adorable.

"He's really sweet." I stuff my hands in the front pocket of his hoodie. "And he's a really good basketball player, too."

Cole's eyes narrow. "Sounds like someone I know."

"He's super funny." I crook my middle and forefinger. "He's also a self-proclaimed flip cup champion."

His shoulders collapse a little.

"Hella smart. Hella sexy. Has a successful career as an architect."

Cole's body seems to grow with every breath he struggles to take. "This pretend guy got a name?"

"Cole. He's on Insta if you want to see pics."

He doesn't laugh. He doesn't move. Hell, I don't even think he's blinked throughout this whole conversation. "So, this Cole guy thought it was okay to just…" He saunters closer to me. "Leave the love of his life in another part of the fucking country all this time?"

"That was my choice," I assure him, running my hands up his arms to curl around his neck. "He fought me about it, but in the end gave me what I wanted. What I needed."

He makes this choking noise that sounds like I just broke his heart a little bit. Or maybe that's my own heart I hear cracking in half. "I'm so sorry I wasn't able to be what you deserved then, Cole. And I'm sorry I didn't come to you and tell you everything before I left."

He shakes his head. "No more saying sorry, Haley." His gaze drags down my body, landing on the faded logo of the hoodie. "We're right where we belong now."

I hope he's right.

"And never think for a second that you were ever undeserving, Haley, of me or of anything else you've ever wanted."

We'll probably never see eye-to-eye about that, but I appreciate him saying it. He means it, which helps me fortify the mental and emotional work I've done on myself.

"You're home to me, Cole."

The way his expression softens lets me know he understands what I'm saying.

I've never had a home before. Not one that lasted more than a year, and never one that was truly *mine*. He also knows that I've lived in a car, a tent, on other people's couches, and in disgusting rentals growing up. Outside of a public library, my dorm room was the closest thing I'd had to a safe place to rest my head at night.

Hell, I didn't know what a home *was* until I spent Thanksgiving with Cole's family senior year. I'd broken down in the car on the way back to campus and confessed that I wanted what he has.

A family.

Roots.

I just had no clue how to attain any of it.

And I wasn't worthy.

Back then, Cole consoled me, but it was something he couldn't relate to. I'm glad. I wouldn't wish my upbringing on my worst enemy. Looking back, that Thanksgiving trip to his family's home was a tipping point for me. I felt like garbage in the center of a sanctuary. Cole's world and mine didn't belong in the same galaxy. Nothing he said could change my mind about it.

That Christmas, I gave him a present to change my feelings about my place in his life. I wore a bracelet and told him I'd be his fucktoy for two solid weeks. When the bracelet came off, the fantasy was over. It was the best two weeks of my life.

I didn't feel like garbage. I didn't feel used.

I felt wanted. Needed.

From the moment I met Cole, until the day before I left him, was the happiest, greatest time of my entire existence. Does he know how much he means to me now? The words, *I love you*, perch on the tip of my tongue. I open my mouth to say it, but it doesn't feel good enough.

Love is too weak for what I feel for this man.

What even is love anyway? I don't know. With my parents, love was an obligation. They're my mom and dad, of course I'm supposed to love them. It didn't matter how they treated me. I'd make excuse after excuse for them until I couldn't take it anymore. Then I ran and cut all connections.

If love is what I run away from, then yeah, maybe I do know love. I ran away from Cole once, too, didn't I?

Maybe. Yes. Hell, I don't know.

What I feel for Cole can't be *only* love. It's too strong, too alive, too endless to be that simple. He's not an obligation. He's not a fantasy.

He's home.

Cole is the familiar, comfortable, wonderful safety I've needed my entire life. He's fun and smart and sweet and generous. He doesn't look down on me or treat me like shit if I do something that disappoints him. He's the goal I've worked towards for the better part of five years. I didn't run away from Cole; I ran away from the girl I was, so I could find the woman who deserved a man like Cole.

I needed to fight, to heal, to grow.

Cole glances at the notes taped all over the bookshelf. "I knew it hadn't been easy for you." He gulps. "But I didn't realize how bad it truly was, Haley."

Now he does.

Cole cups my face, running his thumb along my cheek. I hear what he's not saying. Cole would have helped me through my bad times if I'd let him. He would have supported me however I needed it. He would have done a lot for us both, if only I hadn't run away. What he might not realize is that he helped me break out of my shell all those years ago. He showed me it's okay to want things that may look out of my reach. He gave me hope that I'm not as awful as my parents made me feel all the time.

His gaze locks on mine, making my heart gallop. "You've crawled through Hell, haven't you, Angel?"

"I still am." Dropping to my knees, I hope he understands how much I need him. "Only now, I like it." I'll happily crawl through Hell if Cole's my final destination.

"God *dayem*."

The threads of tension binding us start snapping, one by one. I look up at him with my brow arched and a smile on my face. Cole slowly backs up, each step he takes is another tension line snapping free until the air between us is light and exciting again. His back eventually hits the bay window and he crooks his finger, beckoning me to him.

I don't need a bracelet, collar, or a leash to bring me to my knees for this man.

It's not only a pleasure, but a motherfucking honor.

With my eyes locked on his, I crawl towards him and kneel at his feet. "What do you want?"

Chapter 14

Cole

"What do you want?" she asks me.

What a loaded motherfucking question. I want everything.

I want to rip my hoodie off her sweet body, fuck her until she passes out, and then keep fucking her until my cum drips from between her sweet, thick thighs and then I want to spank her ass until she can't sit. I want to make her crawl on the floor while she begs for me to let her suck my cock. I want to fuck her tits.

I want to pick her up and hold her until she molds against my body and we become inseparable. I want to tell her I'm proud of the work she's done and what she's still doing for herself. I want to hunt her parents down and beat the shit out of them for fucking my girl's head up so much. I want to hug the librarians who gave her a sanctuary. I want to turn back time and give my girl a better life than the one she's lived so far.

I want to love her until the day I die.

I want to worship her. Spoil her. Protect her. Keep her.

"Spread your legs for me." I barely recognize the man I am right now. Gone is my go-easy attitude. Hello, feral. "Lift my hoodie up so I can see your pussy."

"*Your* hoodie?" Haley spreads her thighs, flashing me her pink panties. "Possession's nine tenths of the law, Cole. This sucker belongs to me."

Dropping down to be eye-level with her, I run my finger along the seam of her underwear. The fabric's damp from her pussy already. "And who do *you* belong to, Angel?"

"You, Daddy." She leans back on her elbows, casting me a gorgeous smile.

"That's right." Hooking my finger under her panties, I pull them off and hold them to my nose. Holy fuck she smells good. Dying for a taste, I lower down and drag my tongue along her sensitive flesh.

Her moans are music to my ears.

Shoving my hands under her ass, I lift her up so I can eat my meal properly. Haley hooks her legs over my shoulders, and I've got her half upside down by the time she's melting on my tongue. Haley tastes tart and sweet. Keeping her steady, I assault her clit with my mouth, alternating between licks and sucks until my girl's writhing for me.

"I'm so close. Don't stop."

No problem. Tightening my grip, I hoist her a little higher until she's nearly tipping upside down in my arms. Her ragged breaths saw out of her sweet mouth, faster, faster, faster.

Then she explodes. Haley's hips grind against my mouth and chin as she rides out her beautiful release.

Gently lowering her down, I don't take my hands off her yet. "Give me more."

Going back for seconds, I eat her pussy like it's my last motherfucking meal. Haley's hands fly to my head, holding me in place. Her hips gyrate against my face while she takes what she needs from me. I shove a finger inside her, relishing how tight and soaked she is.

"Oh my God," she cries out, coming again.

I make sure to lick every drop of her pleasure before I stop. "Such a good girl."

Crawling up her sweet body, I shove the hoodie up so I can play with her tits. Sucking one nipple into my mouth, I play roughly with the other, loving how she squirms for me. "Take this thing off. I don't want any barriers between us. I need every inch of you."

My girl's cheeks are splotchy and red. Her eyes are heavy-lidded too. Haley's a perfect combo of precious and powerful. Sweet and seductive. Strong and submissive. She slips out of our hoodie and tosses it to the side.

"Put your hands behind your back, Angel." I tie them together with her panties. After placing an open mouth kiss on her neck, I stand up. "Show Daddy how good you suck cock."

My heart slams against my chest while I pull my dick out, and Haley opens her mouth for me. She greedily licks the pre-cum off the tip.

"Deep throat me, Angel. I want to hear you gag."

I'm halfway in when the head of my cock hits the back of her throat. Haley's nostrils flare and her eyes water as she holds this position and looks up at me. Her gag reflex kicks in.

"Easy, Angel." Burying my hand in her hair, I hold her steady. "Breathe through your nose and keep your tongue flat." Widening my stance, so I'm a little lower, it forces my girl to lean forward. "That's it. Good job."

She struggles to stay balanced with her hands tied behind her, so I hold her shoulder with one hand and place my other on her head. "Daddy's going to fuck your pretty face now."

With her tipped like this, I can reach further down her throat. Another two inches sinks into her mouth. Slurping noises follow.

Christ, why does that sound always get me going? The sloppier the blowjob, the happier the man. I will die on this hill.

My thrusts quicken, even though I stay mindful of how hard I am. The last thing I want is to damage her throat. "You take my dick so well. You're such a slut for my cock, aren't you, Angel?"

She sucks me off harder.

My toes curl. Before I blow my load, I pull

out and step back, stroking myself. "Spread your legs."

Haley's knees scrape the floor as she widens her thighs. Staring up at me like I'm a fucking god, she says, "Come on me, Daddy. Cover me with it."

Pumping my shaft, heat blooms down my back. My release hits hard. Ropes of cum splatter all over her face, tits, belly, pussy. I make a fucking mess all over her.

"Free yourself, Angel." Her binds are easy to get out of. When she wiggles her wrists free, she pitches forward and immediately goes for my dick. Pumping it with both hands, she sucks on the head, trying to get every last drop out of me.

Holy fuuuuuuck. I'm too sensitive for this. I can't... shit... I—

"Hold still," she orders. Haley sucks my tip between her lips, running her tongue along the underside like it's some kind of pacifier.

"Jesus fucking Christ," I groan. "You're gonna break me."

She twirls her tongue around me, enjoying how unraveled I am.

"Enough." I back away because if I don't put a stop to this, I'll tear her open with how hard I want to fuck her.

Giggling, Haley runs her hand over her tits and gathers some of my cum on her fingertips. Then she licks them clean. "I love the taste of you."

Wiping her cheek off with my thumb, I stare down at her for a long moment. All my words catch in my throat. Before I can get my brain to sync up with my heart and mouth, Haley stands and picks her hoodie up.

"Stay?" she asks in a little voice.

I'll stay forever. She only has to ask nicely. Nodding, I lift my pants over my hips and tuck my cock away. "Should I order dinner for us?"

"I can cook something."

She can cook? That's new. "Whatever you want to do is fine with me, Angel."

With a smile, Haley turns to walk away from me. My instincts kick in and I snatch her arm, pulling her back into my chest. Our mouths clash and I kiss her like I'm devouring her. It's possessive. Aggressive.

Desperate.

She presses against my shoulders, pushing me back. "I need food if you plan to spoil me with another round of that big dick, Cole."

Right. Food. Water. She needs nourishment before I deplete her.

"I'll order delivery." Haley doesn't need to cook for me tonight. I'd rather she relax in my arms instead. Wrapping my arm around her waist, I kiss her neck in lazy, open mouth kisses while I pull up Door Dash on my cell. "What do you want?"

"You."

I smack her ass. "I mean for food."

"Still you."

I nip her neck. "*Angel*."

"Smoked brisket, fries, and mac and cheese from Dave's smokehouse, please."

That's more like it. "Good girl." And she used her manners so well too. She just earned a few extra orgasms for doing such a good job.

Making quick work of putting in our order, I toss my cell onto the sofa and get back to using both hands on Haley. Fuck, she's so sexy. And still so messy. "I want you covered in my cum all night. Don't wash it off."

"Yes, Daddy."

She's gonna be the death of me. I don't remember her being this easily submissive before.

Then again, I didn't use to be this dominant. *And I've barely started with her.*

My gaze roams around her apartment, landing on the massive pile of boxes stacked in the dining area. She must eat on the couch or at the counter because there isn't any other place to sit and have a meal here. "What's all that over there?"

Part of me fears it's a bunch of her personal shit she hasn't bothered to unpack. And that stems from the stories she used to tell me about how she never even bothered to take her clothes out of her duffel bag when she was in high school because unpacking meant she was staying and that never happened.

"Event paraphernalia." She flicks her wrist in a *don't worry about all that* kind of way. "Vases, candles, condoms, chalk, ribbons. It's a whole thing."

"Back up. Did you say condoms and chalk?"

"Oh yeah. For emergencies."

"The fuck kind of emergency requires those two things?"

Haley laughs. "You'd be surprised at how many weddings I've planned where a groomsman or bridesmaid wanted to go off for a quickie and needed a condom."

No way.

"And the chalk is what I use in a pinch if the bride gets something on her dress. It doesn't always work, but I can usually hide a stain with it."

No shit. "Clever girl."

She shrugs. "I've learned a few tricks over the years."

I'm so goddamn proud of her for going all in with her event planning talent. She's a natural creative, has great energy, and it's obvious she loves her job. "I can't wait to see you soar, Haley."

"Aww." She shoots me a sweet smile. "Thanks."

The fact that she's standing stark naked, covered in my jizz, while we're having such a sweet convo kills me. It's perfectly us.

And it turns me on like crazy.

Towering over her, I lift her chin and kiss

her lazily while forcing her to walk backwards. Steering her all the way to the door, I drop to my knees. "Put your foot on my shoulder and listen for the delivery."

"Cole," she squeaks. "Wait. I can't—"

"Shut up and do what you're told, Angel." I shove a finger inside her pussy. "Or I'ma put you over my knee and spank your ass until it's too sore to sit on."

Her inner walls clamp on my finger at my threat.

I take my good old time with her—teasing, edging, getting her to the point when she's shaking against the door.

Then someone knocks.

"Tell them you're coming," I say, before latching onto her clit.

"I'm... I... *fuck*." Haley panics. "I'm coming!"

I make sure she's not a liar. Fingering her while I eat her sweet pussy, I make my girl explode with the delivery man on the other side of the door.

"Oh my *God*, Cole."

Guess she doesn't care that they can hear her. Good.

My girl gushes around my finger, coating my mouth and chin with her cum. The instant she's done, I stand and gently push her away from the door so I can answer it.

"Thanks for waiting." I flash the guy a big

smile, knowing that my lips are glistening from my girl's pleasure. "Had to have my dessert first."

The delivery dude gawks at me.

Haley lets out a little squeak, staying out of his sight, still naked and panting like the needy little slut I love.

I snag the bag from him and wink, then shut the door and tip my head to the couch. "You're gonna sit on my lap and let me feed you."

She gives me the same look the delivery guy did.

"Don't make me repeat myself, Angel. You won't like the punishment."

Her eyebrows raise. "Are you threatening me with a good time, Daddy?"

"Dick and orgasm denial sound fun to you?"

She rushes over to the couch and plops down.

"Yeah." I arch a brow at her. "That's what I thought."

Chapter 15

Haley

I didn't get much sleep last night. Or the night before. Or the night before that. Cole and I work all day, sext in between meetings, and hook up at either my place or his to fuck all night.

It's been insane.

My body aches constantly. I'm exhausted all day long, only to catch an energy boost the instant we're together. My brain straddles fantasies of when we'll see each other next and tackling my long list of To Dos for work.

I couldn't be happier.

Tonight, we're meeting at a gym. He's playing basketball with some of his friends, and I want to watch. I can't wait to see that man dunk. I've been giddy about it all day because watching Cole play ball is so damn fun. I was never on a team, but shooting hoops was something I could do alone at a playground after school. I loved it.

Still do, actually.

Chin deep in wedding ideas for my bride Courtney, my cell goes off.

"Hey, Chica. How's it going?"

"Pretty good." I add another pin to my board. "You?"

Jenna blabs about how busy life is and that I need to make a trip to Colorado to see her soon. "I will. Promise."

"Good. How's Cole?"

"Wonderful."

She squeals. "I'm so happy for you."

I'm happy for me, too. It's a weird feeling. "I'm actually going over some ideas for your cousin's wedding right now."

"Ohhh, bet it's gonna be gorgeous."

"She went from mountain wedding to beach."

"Not surprising." Jenna sighs. "Okay, well, I gotta go. Just wanted to check in and say hi. Bye, babe."

"Bye."

Jenna makes calls like this all the time. I used to think it was part of her master plan to wear me down, but I eventually realized it's how she likes to stay connected. I honestly look forward to her calling me.

My phone buzzes with an incoming text.

Cole: Thanksgiving is coming up. Come home with me.

Ummm. Last time I went home with him was a long time ago. Being with his family is still one of the best memories I've ever made, but...

Haley: Are you sure? Won't it be weird?

Little bubbles pop up immediately.

Cole: Do you think I'd ever put you in an uncomfortable situation, Angel?

Every time he calls me Angel, it strengthens my trust in him. I don't get why, but it's how I must be wired.

Haley: No.

Cole: Glad you know that.

My palms grow clammy as I stare at the screen, waiting for him to say something else.

Cole: We don't have to stay the entire weekend.

I'm still at a loss for what to say.

Cole: Think about it and let me know.

I could tell him I have too much work to do and can't afford the time away from my laptop. I could tell him I don't think we should take such a big step so soon. I could tell him lots of things, but they'd all be sorry ass, stupid excuses, and I'm not about to tarnish the progress we've made.

I text him a thumbs up.

Yup. A thumbs up. Ugh, how awkward is that?

The rest of my afternoon takes forever to get through. I hyper-focus on every task, getting through orders, calls, and deep diving into Pinterest until my eyes feel like they're going to bleed. My alarm goes off, yanking me out of my trance, and I shut my laptop down. Part of my personal time management plan is setting alarms for myself, so I don't sink too deep into rabbit holes like Pinterest boards and DIY YouTube videos. Being creative also means time doesn't exist unless I make it.

Hence the alarms.

Stretching my limbs, I get dressed in leggings, a tank top, and a hoodie and slip on my sneakers.

By the time I reach the gym, it's almost seven and I catch the distinct sound of shoes squeaking on the court. Tightening my ponytail, I head in and spot Cole immediately.

He's the sexiest guy on the court.

With a smile plastered on his face, he boxes out his opponent. The guy spins around him and makes a layup.

"Lucky break." Cole points at me. "I was distracted." He jogs over to me, shirt drenched in sweat. "Hey gorgeous." He wraps his arms around me and lifts me off the floor, kissing me.

"Get a fucking room!" someone yells at us.

Cole laces our hands together and pulls me onto the court. "Let me introduce you to some of my boys. That's Dante." He points at a lanky man with a big smile. "That's Jaedyn. We work together." Jaedyn gives a half wave. "And this loudmouth ugly fuck is Josh."

Josh's brows dig down. "I'm not a loudmouth."

"But you are ugly," Jaedyn teases.

"That's not what your mom said last night."

Cole swings his attention back to me. "We're almost done."

Wait. What? Panic punches my heart. "Am I late?" Holy crap. I'd set my alarm and everything so I wouldn't miss this.

"Naw, dipshit here double-booked himself." He hooks his thumb at Jaedyn. "We met a little earlier than we were supposed to. I didn't tell you because I didn't want to derail your day."

My heart falls. "I wouldn't have minded."

"I know, but you have to stay focused." He cups my chin and gives me a warm smile. "Have a seat, Angel."

Confused with how to feel about it, I sit on a bleacher. There are eight full courts in this large space, and only three are being used. It looks like there's also a big track on the second level. This sports complex is huge.

It doesn't take long for Cole to entrance me. The way he dribbles, pump fakes, shoots. He makes getting a basket look effortless. The guys rib on each other the whole time and occasionally Cole points his finger at me and smiles. He's so happy here. He's so happy *period*.

Easy going, funny, and charismatic, Cole could make friends and build a life anywhere he goes.

I envy him that.

It's hard to believe the man on the court right now, goofing off with his friends, is the same person who wore a mask and fucked me into oblivion last night while I wore a collar and leash around my neck.

"Haley!" Cole yells, pulling me out of my thoughts.

All four guys are staring at me, and Cole crooks his finger.

I'm feeling a little bratty. "You'll have to finger harder than that if you want me to come." I lean back on the bleacher, suddenly eager to get him riled up. I don't care if his friends see or not.

This is payback for that Door Dash episode the other night.

"Damn," Josh says, cupping his mouth.

Cole bites his bottom lip and swaggers over to me. Climbing to the top of the bleachers, he towers over me. "Well played."

"Thanks."

"That will cost you later."

I sure hope so.

Grabbing my arms, he puts me over his shoulder and spanks my ass while carrying me down to the court. When I'm back on my feet, he's got this huge smile on his face again, clearly happy with himself. "You're on my team."

His words barely register when Jaedyn tosses me the ball. "Thanks, Haley." He waves goodbye and grabs his coat and bag from the bleacher.

"What? No way. I can't play."

"Why not?" Cole asks. "You're dressed for it."

"I…" Hold up. Why not? I'm nowhere near as good as he is, but I don't suck. "I'm not warmed up."

Cole grabs Dante and Josh by their shirts and drags them backwards. "Start shooting, gorgeous."

My hands are clammy as I palm the ball and dribble it a few times. Running under the basket, I try for a layup and miss the first two. My cheeks heat. This is going to be so bad. Third time, I get it though. Then I back up and shoot again.

"In the bucket," Cole announces in a hilarious voice.

I dribble a little more and shoot again and again, not missing either one.

"There she is." He claps loudly. "Get it, girl!"

Shew, I'm hot. Stripping off my hoodie and tossing it towards the bleachers, I re-focus. Standing at the three-point line, elbow tucked, I shoot.

And sink the ball.

"That's what I'm talking about!" Cole pats Josh on the back. "Let's do this."

Adrenaline pumps in my veins while we play. I swear Cole moves in slow motion whenever I need to pass him the ball, and he speeds up when he shoots it. He's a million times better than I am, but I make three baskets and get six steals.

I'm sure they're going easy on me, but I don't care. This is the most fun I've had in a while. By the time we're done, I'm sweaty and out of breath, with a huge grin on my face.

"Ayyyy!" Cole rushes at me and picks up me, twirling me in the air. "We won!"

"We're not even keeping score," Josh says, laughing.

"You weren't because you'd be depressed knowing what a loser you are," Cole shoots back. "But I always keep score."

Dante wipes his sweat off with his shirt. "Good game."

"Same time next week?" Josh asks.

"I don't think that'll be a problem." Cole looks down at me. "Unless you're busy?"

Ummm. What should I say? Do they really want me to play with them again? I wasn't *that* good. "I'm free."

"You're on my team then," Dante says. "Josh and Jaedyn can fight over Cole."

"Fuck that." Cole takes a bottled water from Josh and hands it to me instead of drinking it himself. "She's all mine."

"Oh, we know." Dante laughs. "She's all you've talked about."

Cole doesn't even have the decency to deny it.

Josh and Dante pack up and head out. I swing my hips with my hands clasped behind my back. "You talk about me?"

"And think about you." Cole swaggers closer. "And dream about you. And jerk off to fantasies about you."

"You have no shame."

"None." He picks the basketball up and dribbles it between his legs while walking backwards. "Have you thought about Thanksgiving?"

"Yes," I say, cautiously. "But it all depends on what happens right here, right now."

He stops dribbling and holds the ball against his hip. "Oh yeah?"

"We're playing PIG. If you win, I'll go. If I win, I'll go."

"This is a good game. I like this game."

"But there's a catch." I hold my finger up. "For every basket you miss, you have to give me an orgasm. And for every basket I miss, I'll be your fucktoy for a day."

"I *really* like this game." Cole tosses the ball over his shoulder without looking, and it bounces off the rim. A wicked grin spreads across his handsome face. "Oops."

Game. On.

Chapter 16

Cole

The next two weeks pass in a blur of fucking, working, and catching some Zzzs whenever possible. I'm not sure how Haley and I bounced back into our old ways so seamlessly, but it's been incredible. I think we're straddling the line of making up for lost time and picking up where we left off.

Part of me has always kicked myself for not chasing her down sooner. Hell, I should have ran after her when she drove off after graduation. I should have told her I loved her from the moment I first knew. I should have done lots of things, but I don't think I was ready for any of it back then.

I'm more than ready now.

Pulling up our text thread, I shoot her a message.

Cole: I want you again.

We fucked twice this morning before I left for work. Walking out her door was crazy hard to do—especially with how adorable she was tangled in her bedsheets with her hair a knotty mess and bare ass red with my handprints.

Haley: You're obsessed.

She's not wrong. This woman's a drug, and I'm completely addicted.

Cole: Show me what I'm coming home to tonight.

Another text comes through while I wait for Haley's reply.

Trey: You coming to Thanksgiving?

Cole: Yes.

Trey: Good. Reid's skipping.

Damn. Our baby brother works way too much, and for him to miss a family tradition makes it so much worse. He needs to simmer down and touch grass once in a while.

Cole: Should we kidnap him?

Trey: Thinking about it.

My cell vibrates again with a series of photos coming through from Haley. Holy shhhhiiiit. First one is her sucking her middle finger, those plump pink lips of hers wrapping around the digit just like they do my cock. Blood rushes to my dick immediately. The second is of her in my hoodie, her hand up around her neck, the other tugging the hem of the hoodie down between her legs. The third is the showstopper. She's standing above her phone, giving me the best view of her pert ass and delicious pussy.

I can barely breathe.

Haley: Your turn, Daddy.

Fuuuuuck.

Looking around to make sure no one can see

into my fishbowl office, I quickly unbuckle my pants and whip out my hard-on. Angling the camera just right, I snap a photo and—

"Noah wants us in his off—shit, sorry." Jaedyn ducks out so fast, I'm left with my dick in one hand, cell in the other, and humiliation skating up my spine. I drop my cell on the floor, yank up my pants, and try to put myself back together behind my desk. Shit, shit, shit. That was so stupid of me.

Grabbing my cell again, I quickly smash a few buttons, shove it in my pocket, and hurry the hell out of my office. I catch up with Jaedyn quickly. "It's not what you think."

"If you were just sending a dick pic to your girl, then it's exactly what I think." He looks straight ahead.

Let's change the subject. "What do you think Noah wants to talk about?"

My cell vibrates in my pocket, and I ignore it. The last thing I need is to see what kind of sexy reply Haley sent me because my dick can't be hard during a meeting with my fucking boss.

"Maybe it's Christmas bonus time?"

"Yeah, maybe." But my gut says it's something else. "Do you think they've made a decision on the Marine Life building?"

"Bro, way too soon for that. I wouldn't plan on hearing from them for a few months. I'm sure architects all over the tri-state area have submitted for consideration."

True. And it's not like I'm holding out to get the contract either, it's just that I'm...

Okay, fine. I'm hopeful this will be my big break. A guy can dream, right?

My cell buzzes again.

"You gonna answer her?" Jaedyn asks, not bothering to hide his smile.

"I will after this meeting. She can wait." My cell buzzes again.

Jaedyn side-eyes me. "She sounds like she can't wait at all."

I push open Noah's door and head in first. Three others are already waiting with notepads and files in front of them. Shit, it's a staff meeting. How the hell did I forget something like that?

And how did Jaedyn?

Noah shuffles papers on his desk, gracing us with a flick of his gaze before grabbing his coffee mug. "Have a seat, gentlemen."

Jaedyn and I drop down in the remaining two chairs at the large table, empty-handed.

Noah strides over. "Let's get started. Brent, where are we with the McDowells?"

"Contract's signed and construction has started."

"Good. Avery, what's on your end?"

"I'm just waiting on a few approvals, but don't expect anything until after the New Year. I also made adjustments for each of the Clyde-Smith projects. They've signed off on them already."

Avery is the favorite in the company. He seems annoyed all the time, but he's a really good goddamn architect who I think just hates people. He also reminds me of my baby brother with how he's always working.

We take turns going around the table, reporting to Noah about shit that could have all been done through email.

My cell buzzes again. *Damnit.*

"Cole?"

I look across the table and lean back in my chair. "All good on my end. Just waiting on some approvals."

"And the party plans? How are those coming along?"

"Good." I perk up, suddenly eager to throw my girl some well-earned credit. "Haley's secured a venue and has already taken care of everything."

Noah's brow arches. "It's two weeks away, so I would hope she has, for fuck's sake."

I want to punch my boss in the mouth. What an arrogant piece of shit. He threw that event at me last minute, and for Haley to get it all together so fast was no small feat. The asshole should be more appreciative.

"Did she sign off on her office design?" Noah asks.

Wait. Woah. Shit. I forgot Noah knew Haley came here asking for a design. I'm not about to tell him I've done it for free. "She's run into a minor hiccup with her landlord. The project's on hold for the time being."

If I say more, I'll get us both in trouble.

Jaedyn shoots me a quick glare and clears his throat. "Did you happen to hear anything about that Marine Life project yet?"

Noah leans back and swivels in his chair. "As a matter of fact, I have."

I swear, all the blood drains from my body and pools in my shoes. A visceral reaction like this speaks volumes about how much hope I've put into this opportunity.

"That's fast," Avery says, looking at me. Going by the smile on his face, he probably already knows he's gotten the deal. He *always* fucking gets it. I mean, hey, good for him, but damn, I'd like a shot for once too.

Noah stands up and clasps his hands behind his back. Slowly walking around the conference table, he says, "There were fifty-two designs submitted."

My heart drops. Well, there went my last hope. I can't compete with that much talent. I can hardly compete with the people in my office.

"Getting this deal was a long shot," Noah says solemnly. "And I'm really proud of each of you for submitting. You made NGC look damn good."

Just fucking say it. Say we didn't get it. Or say we did, and it's all thanks to Avery.

"Apparently, it came down to three options.

One from Lumineer Architects in San Diego, one from London, and the other," he says, his gaze sailing to Avery, "from our humble office."

My stomach drops. *Avery got it.* I knew he would, and I'm happy for him, but man, I put my *soul* into that design, and it still got me nowhere. Swallowing past the tightness in my throat, I do my best to not let this news affect me. So what if I didn't get it? I'm used to rejection. I'll just try harder next time.

"Congratulations," I say, meaning it. My hands are clammy. I can't believe this news is hitting me so hard. "You deserve it, man. You bust your ass more than anyone else here."

"Who said it was Avery?" Noah glowers at me for a heartbeat. Two heartbeats. Five heartbeats. Then he starts to slow clap.

What the hell?

Everyone else starts clapping, too.

They're all staring at me.

Avery's the first to get up and hold his hand out for me to shake. "You deserve this, man. Well. Fucking. Done."

What's happening?

I look over at Jaedyn. He beams me a huge smile and grips my shoulder, shaking it. "You did it, man."

My hearing gets wonky. I think I'm hallucinating.

Noah walks over and shakes my hand like he's trying to rip it out of the socket. "Great job,

Cole. This is huge for us."

No. Huge for *me*.

"They didn't even hesitate," Noah says proudly. "From what I was told, the board took one look at your design and didn't even bother looking at the rest. They said it was innovative, inspiring, and has a boldness that reflects the spirit of their conservation efforts." He grins. "That's a direct quote."

I can't wrap my head around it. It's surreal.

Standing up to shake everyone's hands, I'm floating on a cloud.

"Alright, alright, everyone. Get back to work." Noah dismisses us so fast, my brain's still catching up with my feet.

Jaedyn steers me out of there and to the front of the office where Tamara waits with this huge, bright smile. "Congrats, Cole!" She hugs me tight and I'm still so dumbfounded, I just hold her.

"Did everyone know about this but me?"

"Oh yeah. We got an email about it this morning saying to keep it a secret until the staff meeting. I ordered you a cake. It's in the fridge." Tamara presses her finger to her lips. "Shhh. I did *not* tell anyone else about that. It's all for you. Coconut with white icing."

"I love you, girl." Giving her another hug, I notice Jaedyn eyeing me like he wants to chew my arms off for some reason.

No way. Pulling back, I narrow my gaze at

Tamara, then at Jaedyn, then back to Tamara. "IWYTCAOMF?" *I want you to come all over my face.*

Her cheeks redden and she smacks Jaedyn's arm. "You told him?"

His eyes grow big. "I didn't tell him anything."

"You're the worst liar." Tamara jabs her finger at me. "Don't tell the boss."

"I would never." I can't believe they're together. Noah will have an aneurysm if he finds out. Office romances are not allowed. "And Jaedyn didn't tell me. I just helped him figure out a few of your, uhhhh, puzzles. That possessive look he just had on his face gave him away."

"Awww." Tamara looks up at him. "IWTSYD."

I go ahead and decode it for him. "I want to suck your d—"

"Got it," Jaedyn says loudly. "Thanks."

"Happy to help." My cell goes off in my pocket. Speaking of sucking dick, what did Haley send me?

Holy shit. Forty-seven messages. What the fuck?

Julian: I'm forever changed. Not cool bro.

Reid: I threw up in my mouth.

Michael: I'm telling mom.

Trey: Hey, if I had to see it, so did all of you. Merry early Christmas, fuckers.

Julian: I'm scarred for life.

Heart racing, I scroll through the texts in the brother group chat. Then I open the one that's just from Trey.

Trey: WHAT THE FUCK! I need to bleach my eyes out now. Thx.

I'm so fucking confused. I have to read it twice and slow down to figure out what's just happened.

Oh. Shit.

I sent the fucking dick pic to Trey, not Haley. And that asshole sent it to the group chat for all my brothers.

I hate him.

Cole: *middle finger emoji*

To the group chat I text: Hey, don't be jealous mine's the biggest.

Trey: It's not. Trust me.

Michael: Ur so precious, bro.

Julian: Aww wittle baby.

Reid: Mine will make a woman skip her next life.

Trey: Yeah, but you gotta break away from your work to find a woman first, bro.

Julian: Amen. And why the fuck aren't you coming to Thanksgiving, Reid?

The chat blows up, the new target being Reid, and I close out of it.

Haley's is the only one left, and it's a picture of her pouting at me.

Haley: You're no fun. I wanted a dick pic, and you left me on read. That's gonna cost you.

I close out of it and tuck my cell back in my pocket. She can make me pay however she wants to. This day is just getting better and better.

"Are you taking off for the rest of the day?" Tamara asks.

"Hell yeah." Hooking my arms around her and Jaedyn, I steer them towards the kitchen. "But first, let's go eat cake."

Chapter 17

Haley

It's only three o'clock, which means I've got probably four more hours before Cole comes home. Just enough time for a nap. This laggy, icky feeling has been creeping in all day. I've been working nonstop lately, so this might be my body telling me to slow down.

Dragging my ass to bed, I climb in and crash.

An hour later, I'm stiff and groggy. My nose is a little stuffy, too. *Damnit.* Pulling the covers over my head, sleep takes me again.

When I wake up a second time, it's to the sound of someone knocking on my door.

Cole. I need to get him a key to my place.

Climbing out of bed, I don't bother fixing my hair or putting on pants. Shuffling to the door, I open it and smile. "Hi."

His face falls. "What's wrong?"

"Nothing." I yawn. "I just woke up."

He presses the back of his hand to my forehead. "You feel warm."

"Probably because I was under three heavy

blankets." I gently knock his arm down. "I'm good. I feel a lot better now that I slept."

He doesn't buy my lie. "You're sick." Coming inside, he looks around and sees that I've been busy all day. "You've run yourself into the ground, Hales."

No, I haven't. It's nothing for me to pull a seventy-hour work week.

"Come on." He scoops me up. "You're getting back into bed."

"I'm fine. Seriously, I feel way better now that I've caught up on my sleep."

Cole looks guilty, as if it's all his fault I haven't rested much lately.

"Chill." I wrap my arms around his neck. "And put me down."

He growls even as he obeys.

"Now," I say, craning my neck to look up at him. "What are you doing home so early?"

A low, heavy sigh leaves him. "I'll feel like a shithead for saying."

"Say it anyway."

Cole runs a hand through his hair. "I had a great day today. One of the best days ever. And I was gonna cash in on my free-use reward." He holds his hand out. "But I'm not doing that if you're feeling sick. I want you rested and healthy."

"Back up." I cross my arms. "What made this the best day ever?"

He looks like he's not comfortable telling

me.

What the hell?

"It can wait. I'd rather you—"

"I'm fine." Time to switch tactics. Walking my fingers up his chest, I unbutton his shirt and run my hands all over him. "Tell me about your day, Daddy." Leaning in, I lick one of his nipples and bite it just enough to make him hiss.

"Fuuuck," he whispers. When he looks down at me, his gaze is darker. "I'm trying to be a good guy here and take care of you."

"So, take care of me." I unbuckle his belt.

Cole snags my hands before I can free his cock. "I'm putting you to bed."

Oh goodie.

When he picks me up again, I imagine how good he's going to rail me tonight. "Tell me your good news."

"Later." Placing me gently on the bed, Cole frowns when he touches my head again. "Shit, Hales. You're burning up."

"It's because I've been hot and bothered all day, waiting for your reply."

His chuckle is half-hearted. "Stay," he says, before leaving my bedroom. He comes back a few minutes later with a mug of tea and a plate of sliced onions.

Eww.

"Uhhh." I give him the side-eye. "What's that for?"

"Your feet." He sets the dish on the side

table. "Where do you keep your socks?"

"I'm not putting onions on my feet. That's gross."

"You will do what you're told, Angel." He finds my sock drawer and pulls out a pair. "Drink your tea."

Pouting, I cross my arms, ignoring how crappy I feel. "Tell me your good news first."

Cole's expression warms. Sitting on the side of the bed, he rests my feet on his lap and massages them. "I worked on a design concept for a new building. It's a Marine Life conservation center. They'll save turtles, coral, and other sea life around Banner Bay."

"That's amazing."

He shakes his head, ducking to hide his pride. Cole never brags about his accomplishments. Not even when he had the highest points scored senior year. His humbleness is adorable. "All my concepts are unconventional. It's held me back." His gaze lifts and deadlocks on mine. "Until today."

My heart stumbles to a stop. "You got it?"

The smile on his face is so huge, it blows me over. "They took one look at my concept and chose me without even looking at the others."

"That's *amazing*!" Excitement surges through me, and I bolt forward to wrap my arms around him. "I'm so proud of you."

He squeezes me back. "Thanks."

"This is huge. We have to celebrate." I've

definitely gotten a second wind. To hell with this cold trying to whoop me. "Let's go somewhere."

"Whoa, whoa, not tonight, Angel." He presses my chest, forcing me to lie back down. "We'll go out once you're feeling better."

"I feel great."

"Well, your cheeks are flushed, and your eyes are a little glassy."

"It's my love for you shining out of my face."

He cracks a loud laugh. "I appreciate that, but you're not going anywhere tonight."

"It's a cold, Cole. Not the plague."

"Well, let's ensure it doesn't turn into something worse." He grabs my foot and starts massaging again. "You're going to listen and do what you're told, or those nine free-use days I got? I'll never use them."

My mouth drops. "You're a cruel, cruel man."

"Cold-hearted to the core," he confirms, rubbing my feet harder. "You should trade me in for someone nicer."

"I'm considering it." Leaning back on my pillows, I sigh. His hands are so big and warm. This foot massage feels incredible. "I'm really proud of you, Cole. You deserve all the good things in life."

He keeps his head down. "So do you."

That hits a little harder than it should. Cole means what he says. And maybe my parents did too, but my man says it from a place of love, while my mom and dad said those same words from a place of jealousy. I stuff the ugly memories back in their box where they belong. I'm never letting the shadows of my past darken any part of my bright future with Cole.

"You've been working too hard, Angel. I know you want to build your business, but you better slow down."

He's right. I'm being impatient, as usual, and busting my ass double time to advertise and network as much as I can. Between hustling at work and spending every spare second I can with Cole, I'm exhausted.

Wouldn't change it for the world, though.

"Everything's set for your party. You're going to love it."

"I know I will." He gestures at the mug on the table. "Drink that."

Grabbing the steamy mug, I try to smell what kind of tea it is. Fumes hit my sinuses and I cough. "What is this?"

"Hot toddy." He takes a disk of sliced onion and… is that plastic wrap? "Hold still." Cole gently places the onion against the sole of my foot and wraps it in saran wrap.

I don't think this onion thing is going to do much more than make my feet smell terrible, but this hot toddy is amazing.

And strong.

"Drink, Angel." He grabs the other onion

disk and places it on my other foot. After wrapping it slowly, he slips on a pair of thick socks.

Warmth spreads through my body as I drain the mug. "Happy?"

"Getting there," he says, kicking off his shoes and crawling into bed with me. When I curl up in his arms and sigh, he kisses my head. "Now I'm happy."

My eyelids grow heavy fast. Between the drink, Cole's body heat, and just having him here with me, I can't keep my eyes open. I crash immediately.

• • •

Okay, hear me out. I don't know if it was the onions, the whiskey in that hot toddy, or the extra sleep I got, but I feel amazing. It's eight o'clock in the morning. Holy crap, I slept a long time. Cole's still out like a light next to me.

How can a guy look hot even when he *sleeps*?

It's just unfair.

I look like a deranged goblin in the morning while he's sex on a stick.

Creeping out of the bed, I dash to the bathroom to unwrap my feet. Forget looking like a goblin. I fucking *smell* like one. These onions are so stinky. I can't believe I let him do this. It also might have worked. My nose isn't even stuffy anymore.

While brushing my teeth, I peek out at Cole. He's still conked out with his arms folded under the pillow, his ass barely covered with my sheets. I'm glad he stayed the night. I'm also sad he had a great day yesterday, and even left work early to come to me, and I crapped out on him.

He rolls over with a moan.

Sweet jeebus, I need to look away before I pounce on him.

Hurrying into the shower, I exfoliate, shave, shampoo, condition and rinse, and by the time I step out, I'm a new woman. Whatever cold I might have been getting is definitely gone. Shit, maybe I wasn't getting sick at all, and it was just exhaustion getting the better of me.

I'm not working longer days than normal, but the time I spend getting projects done has been intense. It feels like my successful career hinges on how well I can execute this party for Cole's company. I did my homework on the client list he gave me for invitations. There are some big names on there. It would be nice to diversify my portfolio and really make a name for myself.

Speaking of which…

I'm so proud of Cole for getting that Marine Life building job. It's about time Cole's inspiring concepts got recognition. I have a feeling, based on what he said yesterday, that Cole didn't think he was going to get it, which makes me wonder if he gets rejected a lot.

My heart sinks.

Cole and I are opposites with tackling a project. He goes all in with his heart and soul. I keep those two things in a box, so if I fail, the pain is barely noticeable. I imagine Cole has faced rejection with his designs many times, and knowing him, he felt each one like a stab in the heart.

As creatives, it's easy to take someone else's vision and translate it to reality for them. It's quite another experience to fashion something from scratch and present it to another, waiting for them to judge it. Accept or reject it.

Cole getting this account isn't just a big break for him. It's validation.

I know how important that is.

After drying off, I quietly crawl back into bed and pull the blankets away from him. Straddling his legs, I bend down and take his length into my mouth. *Hooray for morning wood.*

Cole inhales through his nose. "Mmm." He cracks open his eyes while I lick the pre-cum off his dick. "Morning." He grunts when I try to deep throat him. "Fuck, girl." He presses his hand on my head. "You must be... *fuck*. You must be feeling better."

"Mmm hmm." I pump him with my free hand and suck harder.

"Shhhit." Cole's hips drive upwards so he can fuck my face. "I'm not gonna last long if you..." His breaths turn ragged. "That's it,

166

Angel."

I swear his dick gets bigger in my mouth.

"Don't stop."

I double-down on my efforts.

"You're such a slut for my cock."

I am.

I know he's getting close to a release when a sheen of sweat coats his body. I pop off and jerk him faster. "Give me your cum, Daddy."

"Put your mouth back where it belongs." Cole grabs my hair and holds my head down. I put all my energy into giving him the best, sloppiest, noisiest blowjob ever. "Swallow it," he grits out. "Take it all, Angel."

Cum floods my mouth.

"When I'm done, don't stop sucking."

No problem.

I keep sucking even as his dick softens. Shit, even when he's got a chub, I can't fit the whole thing in my mouth. Cole's huge.

"That's my good girl." He threads his fingers in my wet hair and pulls me off him. "I want to fuck you now."

Cole's got great rebound time.

I straddle his groin, angling his dick against my pussy, when he holds my hips to stop me from sinking down on him. "Condom, Angel."

Right. Wow. How did I let such an important thing slip my mind? Easy.

"I'm on birth control." I got on it after graduation, even though I never slept with another person since Cole.

His jaw ticks. "You want to…" His voice dies out before he finishes that sentence.

"No barriers between us." I lower down on his dick. It takes a hot minute to get him fully seated. "You're fucking huge."

Cole remains quiet, staring at me with hawk eyes while I ride him.

He's so deep, his cock knocks against my cervix every time I bounce. It hurts and feels good at the same time. Flattening my feet on either side of his hips, I lift and rotate my waist until his eyes roll back.

"Holy shit." Cole's hands fly up to the headboard so he can hold on tight. "Ride me, Angel. Take what you need from me."

I shift from a circulating motion to a grinding back and forth one. There's constant friction against my clit this way. My pussy is full. He's hitting some deep pleasure point I can't ever reach on my own. It doesn't take long for my orgasm to build.

Cole tips his head back. "Fuck your Daddy, Angel. Scream for me."

I falter. My thighs shake.

Without warning, he lets go of the headboard, grips my hips, and slams into me until I'm the one holding on for dear life. Our bodies slap together. Sweat beads on my brow and runs down my back. Cole flips us over and thrusts long and hard into me while I lay on my back. "Put your feet on my shoulders, slut."

I can barely breathe when he pounds into me at this angle. It's too much. Too deep. Too—

"Cream on my cock."

He wraps a hand necklace around my throat, and I see stars when I orgasm.

"That's my greedy little cock whore." He slows his pace once I'm done coming. "Squeeze my dick again."

I can't control my body with how languid I've become. "I don't have the strength."

He bites my shoulder. "Do it."

I squeeze, my Kegels barely gripping him because I'm too spent.

"Again."

I obey, but it takes work and concentration.

He grinds against me, rubbing against my clit. "*Again*."

"I can't." I'm dizzy. I came too hard for this.

Cole pinches my nipple, and my body reacts immediately—my cunt clamping down on his dick. "God *damn*, your body responds so well to me, Angel."

"Only for you," I gasp. I think I'm going to come again. "Only ever for you, Daddy." I hold his arms, my nails digging into him while I hold on. "I'm close."

He pulls out and attacks my clit with his tongue. He makes me come one more time and then jerks himself until he unloads all over my swollen pussy. Then he shoves inside me again and keeps us locked together until he's flaccid.

"That was…" His heart pounds against my chest. When he lifts off me, he frowns. "Dangerous."

"No." I pull him closer so I can kiss him. "That was perfect." With a smile, I wrap my legs around his middle and keep him against me. Inside me. "Want this to be day one of your free use?"

Chapter 18

Cole

Free-use, day one: I fucked Haley's tits twice, and her sweet pussy so many times, she couldn't walk to the kitchen to get a snack afterwards.

Day two, I made her meet me in a clothing store where she sucked me off in a dressing room. Then we went out for dinner, where I fingered her under the table while she ate cheesecake for dessert. I locked us in the bathroom after we paid our bill and railed her against the sink.

Day three, I fucked her ass at my place. I also fucked her throat until pretty tears streamed down her face. I made her spit my cum out onto her tits so I could smear it all over them and wouldn't let her clean it off for hours.

She's turning me into an animal.

It's day four. "Pull my cock out."

Haley squirms in the passenger seat of my car. "What if we get into an accident and I die with your dick in my mouth?"

I pull onto the shoulder of the highway. "Better?"

"Not hardly," she says, smiling. "But I'll take it."

Cars zoom past us, going eighty miles an hour. I keep an eye out for trouble—and cops. "Start sucking."

She unfastens her seatbelt and I love how her hips and ass fill out her dress as she bends over to blow me. Her hot mouth on my dick will never get old. Every time she takes me like this, I feel it down to my motherfucking toes. Her head bobs in my lap. Slurping noises fill my ears.

I don't want her to finish me off, I just like that she obeys so well. "Stop, Angel." Haley pauses, with my dick halfway down her throat. "That's enough."

She lifts up, looking dejected. "Did I do it wrong?"

"Hell no." I run my thumb across her fat bottom lip. Jesus, she's so fucking pretty. "I just wanted to feel your hot mouth for a minute." After tucking my dick back in, I look into my side mirror and hop back onto the highway. "Buckle up and take your panties off."

She does as I say.

"Finger yourself." I flick my gaze at her. "Daddy wants to hear all those delicious wet noises."

"Okay," she whispers. Haley shimmies out of her thong and hangs it on my rearview mirror. Propping her feet on the dashboard, she lets her legs fall open and plays with herself. "I want your cock, not my hand."

"You don't get anything until you've earned it, Angel."

"Mmmph." She bites her bottom lip. I bet she's sore from all I've done to her this week. I like knowing she's got an ache from me. If it was a problem, she'd say something. Since she hasn't, I'm going to keep going. "I'm so swollen."

"Needy little cunt of yours wants my cock again, doesn't it?"

"Yes." Wet noises fill the car. She's soaked. "I need you, Daddy."

"Put three fingers inside. I want you stuffed."

She squeaks at my demand and complies. Her breath hitches. "It's not enough."

Pulling off on an exit, I park in the back of a grocery store lot while she keeps masturbating for me. "Get out."

If she wants to deny my request, she keeps it to herself. I watch my beautiful girl collect her confidence and swing the car door open.

Good girl.

She trusts that I'll keep her safe — and that includes making sure we don't get caught.

There's no one else here because the store is closed for the holiday, and I've parked us in the back corner where there are plenty of trees and bushes.

We just have to make this quick, so we don't push our luck.

"Hands on the hood."

She leans forward, her palms firmly planted on my car. I lift her dark green dress up over her hips, running my hand along her ass. *Smack*! I spank her once, loving the handprint that blooms on her delicate skin. "So fucking pretty." I nudge her legs a little wider and pull my dick out. "Beg for my cock, Angel."

"Please, give it to me, Daddy. I need it."

Teasing her, I rub the head of my dick along her folds, loving how wet she is.

"Come inside me." She looks over her shoulder at me. "Please."

My heart stops. We haven't gone that far yet.

"You'll take whatever I give you." I push into her. "Now thank your Daddy."

"Thank you, Daddy."

Every time I slide into her, she feels so good. It scrambles my grey matter. I want to fill her up. I want my cum dripping out of her all day long. I want to wife her up.

It doesn't take long before my orgasm barrels down on me. I pull out and come all over her ass cheeks. "Stay." Tucking my dick back in my pants, I jog over to the passenger side and retrieve napkins from my glove box. Gently wiping off my mess, I give her one more quick little spank. "Thank me."

"Thank you, Daddy."

I spin her around. "For what?"

"Fucking me so good." I cock a brow at her while lifting her onto the hood of my car. Silently placing her feet on my shoulders, I eat her pussy like it's my goddamn dinner. She cries out my name, her thighs clamping down on my ears when she comes. "Cole!"

I know it's good when the honorifics vanish. I love it.

Sinking two fingers inside her, I hit Haley's cervix, running my fingers along that tender flesh until she's gasping. "Say my name again."

"Cole." Her eyes roll back. Her body tenses. The wet noises coming from her cunt are so damn loud, I might just come in my pants hearing it. I finger her harder. "That's it, Angel. Let go. Push out for me."

"I'm going to—"

She squirts all over my hand.

"That's my good girl." I lean in and kiss her sweet mouth. "Now get back in the car before I fuck your ass."

She stalls out and I almost think she's going to stay put just to test me. But then she slides off the hood of my car and wobbles back to the passenger side door with her dress still over her hips. My girl drops back into her seat and grabs her thong from the mirror.

I slam my hand on the hood of my car and shake my head.

Those are staying right where they are.

Chapter 19

Haley

My body is so boneless, I have no clue how I'm supposed to get through Thanksgiving dinner with his family. The next two hours go by in a blur, and before I know it, we're pulling into a long driveway.

I have a flashback to the first time I met his parents. How on earth can a single turn into a driveway feel this good, this solid, this safe and perfect? Warmth spreads through my chest, followed quickly by panic.

"What if they don't want me here?" I ask quietly. It's too late to turn back now.

"Haley." Cole's warning is clear. He'd never put me in a position like that.

I slump in my seat. My stomach twists. "What if they hate me now?"

"They have no reason to hate you for anything." His big hand falls to my thigh, and he gives it a squeeze. "Trust me."

I'd hate me if I were them. I ditched Cole and didn't look back. Guilt grips my heart, squeezing it to a pulp. I feel vulnerable and terrible. I reach up to snag my thong from the mirror. Cole catches my hand and shakes his head. "I told you they stay where they are."

"Please?" I beg.

He shakes his head again. "I like them hanging there."

"Well, I like being completely dressed before I see your mom." *Who may or may not want to beat me to death with her wooden spoon.* Dread consumes me. Why did I agree to come here? It's too soon for this. Burying my head in my hands, I try to reel in my emotions that are escaping their bottle.

"Hey." Cole's tone softens. "Look at me, baby."

I do and don't like his expression. "I feel sick."

"I'll never ever put you in the line of fire. Not even with my family. They love you, Hales." He grabs my hand and kisses it.

Tears fill my eyes, making Cole all blurry. "I wasted so much time, didn't I?"

"You took what you needed." He taps my nose and shoots me a smile. "Now, be my good girl and let me bring you home to your family."

His words barely process in my warped brain before he's opening the door for me. I'm still in panic mode. Shit. I... I can't... "Cole."

"I gotchu." He grabs my hand and pulls me out. "Come on, Angel."

The outside of the house is exactly like I

remember it. It's as if these past five years didn't exist. I'm right back to the first time I came here for turkey and Miss Ellie's famous apple pie. Cole laces his fingers with mine and we climb the porch steps. There's a big wreath on the red door that has a ribbon on it covered with sunflowers.

Cole squeezes my hand before opening the front door. Warm air, pumpkin, and something inexplicably wonderful hits my nose. "Mama, we're home!"

Two dogs barrel towards us, tails wagging and tongues out. I let go of Cole so I can pet them. "Pete and Zeb?"

"Zeb passed. This is one of his bastard children," Cole says, giving the dogs a good head rub.

"Ohhhh!" The sound of Miss Ellie's voice startles my heart. She rushes towards us, wiping her hands off on her apron.

"Hey, Mama." Cole hugs her tight and they rock back and forth, which is totally an Ellie thing. I've never seen anyone hug the way she does.

Then she looks over at me and my stomach drops. Ellie's face falls. She lets go of her son and calmly walks towards me. It takes all my strength to not cower or back up until my ass hits the door.

Or better yet, turn and sprint the hell out of there before she can reach me.

"Haley." She says it with so much warmth, it's like stepping into sunshine after living in a cold cave. Miss Ellie brings me into a big hug that seeps into my bones. "I knew you'd come back to us." She hug-rocks me too and when I wrap my arms around her, it's like I'm falling apart and staying together at the same time. "Ohhh let me look at you." She pulls away to cup my face. "You get prettier and prettier." She taps my nose. "You keeping my boy in line?"

"Yes, ma'am." I swipe the tears from my eyes.

"He treating you like a gentleman should?"

My smile goes a mile wide. "Yes, ma'am."

"Guess what?" She turns to him. "You're the last ones in."

Cole looks up at the ceiling. "Damnit." He must read my mind because he looks over and explains, "Last ones in have to help with dishes."

Miss Ellie hooks her arm with mine and starts walking. "Come on. I need help in the kitchen, and I bet you could use a break from my son. He talks too much."

"What? No, I don't."

"See what I mean?" Ellie laughs.

"Now I *know* you're done cooking," Cole argues while we walk away from him. "What's she gotta help you with?"

"My wine won't drink itself," she calls out.

We enter her kitchen, where there's enough food to feed the entire state. My gaze lands on a platter. "Are those—"

"My deep-fried stuffing balls? Yes." She

grabs a little plate that's next to the large tray piled high with them. "I made extra just for you, because I know how much you loved them last time you were here."

And just like that, I'm home.

• • •

Dinner is a blast. Crowded around this massive table that stretches from the kitchen to the living room, half of us sit in folded chairs, while the rest get wooden ones. My plate is full. And my heart is too.

I can't believe they welcomed me back into their family so easily. Then again, this is how I think Cole's family is. Everyone is family. Everyone is welcome.

As Cole's dad, Bryan, carves a massive turkey, giving his wife props for cooking such an amazing feast, the front door squeaks open, and the dogs immediately go running.

Ellie stands up, her eyes warm even with the look of shock on her face as her youngest comes into the house. "Reid!"

"Ayyyy." Trey leans back in his chair. "Glad you made it."

Reid pets the dogs and tries to push past them to join us at the table. "Move, dogs." They don't. Tails wagging, they both fight to get head pats from him. "Come on, give me space."

"Good to have you home, son." Bryan glances at Ellie for a moment and they share a look. I have no clue if it's relief or concern.

"Sorry I'm late. Traffic was terrible."

Ellie gives him an enormous hug. "Cole, go get another chair from the basement for your brother."

Cole hops ups and does what he's told. My heart does a weird flip floppy thing as I watch the family interact—picking on each other, passing food, laughing, while Reid makes his way around the table to say hi to everyone. I have a feeling Reid doesn't come home nearly as often as the others do. I wonder why?

"Here ya go." Cole pops the creaky metal folding chair open and puts it next to me. "You get the honors of sitting by my girl."

Reid takes a seat. "I'm Reid." He holds his hand out for me to shake.

Guess he doesn't remember me. Not that I expected him to. "Haley."

His eyes widen. "Wait. *Haley*, Haley?"

"Yeah. Haley, Haley." Cole gives him a look.

Reid's exhaustion shows even when he tosses me a big smile. "It's been a while."

"Yeah. It has." I'm not sure what else to say.

"Guess what?" Cole leans forward to look at his baby brother. "You're on dish duty."

Reid's shoulders slump. "Damn. I forgot about that."

"We'll help," I say, because honestly, Reid looks like he could fall face-first onto his dinner plate from exhaustion. "Won't we, Cole?"

"What? No way."

I smack his arm.

"Okay, fine." Cole places a roll on my plate. "You're lucky she's sweet, bro. I'd have made you suffer."

Reid scoops a huge pile of green bean casserole onto his plate. "I owe you one, Haley."

"So, boys," Bryan says. "Who's got some good news for us?"

The brothers and their significant others take turns sharing great things going on in their lives, but I notice neither Reid nor Cole look like they plan to say a word. In fact, when it's Cole's turn, he just sits back and shrugs. "Same ole, same ole."

Reid nods. "Same ole, same ole."

What? No. "What about your big—"

Cole flicks me a warning look that has me shutting up immediately.

"Your big what?" Ellie presses.

"Nothing," he says, playing it off like he has no clue what I'm talking about.

I can't believe him. Why isn't he telling his family about his big design getting accepted for the Marine Life project?

Chapter 20

Cole

After dinner, everyone breaks off into groups. There's a card table for playing spades and rummy. Dad brought out a bunch of board games, too. Reid, Haley, and I are doing the dishes while Mom takes pictures of everyone else having fun.

"What's going on with you, man?" I take a clean plate from Reid and dry it off.

"Nothing."

"You look like you've been hit by a truck."

"Thanks." He shoves another dripping plate at me.

Haley comes in with more dishes for us to wash, and quietly places them on the counter.

Reid eyes me up. "What's the big news you don't want to share?"

"Don't have any," I lie.

Reid looks over his shoulder at Haley. "Got something to do with her?"

"Nope." I stack the dried plates on the kitchen table and grab another towel from the drawer. "Trey says you've been sleeping in the office."

"Trey needs to mind his business. He doesn't even work in my office anymore, so how would he know?"

Good point, but my guess is he has people checking up on our baby brother.

"How's it coming along in here?" Mom chirps. "Ohhhh, you're almost a third of the way done."

Like that's an accomplishment? "Mama, did you use every dish, pot, and piece of silverware you own?" Because it feels like it.

"Obviously," she says, laughing. Putting her arm around us both, she gives us a squeeze. "It's so wonderful having this house full. I can't wait to have more grandbabies, too."

"Don't look at me." Reid gives her the stink eye. "I'm just a baby."

Mom swings her hopeful gaze to me and raises her eyebrows.

I shake my head. "Nope. Not happening."

I notice Haley pausing at the doorway with a stack of empty platters. When I turn to give her a reassuring look, something passes over her face that I can't read. She bristles and rushes forward with her arms full. "I can't believe we ate everything. There aren't any leftovers." She places them on the counter and fans her reddening face. "Phew, it's hot in here."

The windows are cracked open to let the cold air in, but she's right. It's stifling. My body temp probably has more to do with how good she looks in that dress than the actual heat in the house. I want her again.

I want her always.

"Come for a walk with me," I say, tossing my towel on the counter.

"Hey, no!" Reid panics. "Don't leave me with all this."

"Sorry, not sorry, bro." I grab Haley's hand and pull her out of the kitchen before anyone can stop us.

I'm not worried about leaving him with all the dishes. Even as we dash out the door, Erin and Trey get up from the couch and head into the kitchen to help. Our family is all about teamwork.

"Where are we going?" Haley asks, buttoning up her coat.

"Nowhere special. I just wanted a few minutes alone with you." Steering her over to the trail on the other side of the driveway, I wrap my arms around her waist and frog-walk us a few steps. I think something's up with her, and I want to know what it is. "Did I tell you how beautiful you look today, Angel?"

"Yes, like four times."

"One more can't hurt." I let her go. White puffs leave my mouth each time I exhale. The temp really dropped over the past few hours. "You looked a little caught up in your head back there. What's going through your mind, Hales?"

And there's that body language I know so

well. I'm right. Something's up.

"Nothing at all," she lies. "I'm just admiring what you have, Cole." Her smile is tight. "Your family is amazing."

I'm not sure how to respond. She's not looking for validation of her opinion about my family. This is something deeper. Darker. I try to grab her hand, but she jerks back so I can't touch her.

"Haley," I warn. If she doesn't want to be touched right now, fine. But I can't stop the fear that punches me in the gut when she wraps her arms around herself. She's pulling back from me. *What if she runs again?* "Talk to me."

"Why didn't you tell everyone about your big news, Cole?"

I slow my roll. That's... not where I thought this conversation was going. "It's not time for that yet."

"What do you mean?" Her brow pinches. "What more are you waiting for?"

I don't have an answer.

Haley sighs, her head falling. "I just wanted to see them be proud of you. I wanted to share that with you." Her tears shake me to my core. This isn't about me or my design news. This is something else.

"I want to wait until I'm sure, Hales." My arms ache to hold her. Why is she closing up over something like this? I don't understand what's going on. "I'm not willing to put the cart before the horse. They could change their minds and nix the deal."

"So what?" Her voice shakes. "You did something great. It should be celebrated." Her chin trembles and the first tear falls.

"Hey, whoa." I close the space between us, my heart pounding. "What's going on, Haley?"

"Your family is…" A breath shudders out of her, white puffs fogging the air between us. "Do you have any idea how lucky you are, Cole?"

Ah. I get it now. The problem is, I have no clue what to say about it.

"Everyone's just so supportive and sweet." She looks back at the house. "I…God, what's wrong with me?" She rubs her chest, wincing.

"Nothing's wrong with you, Hales."

She scoffs, letting me know she whole-heartedly disagrees. "I would have given anything to have what you have here."

And just like that, I'm thrown back to the last time she came to dinner at my parent's house…

Our bellies are so full, I swear I'm gonna pop. We're spending the night because the trip home is a long one and nobody's up for that kind of trip after eating their weight in turkey and pie.

"Get in here with me." Haley lifts the covers to my old bed. "I can make you fit."

She said those exact words to me last night too when I fucked her in the ass.

We both cram into my full-sized bed, the old bedframe creaking loudly. I make a *uh oh* face at her and she laughs. It's late. About two am. We've been out on four-wheelers, playing cards, and drinking until most of the family called it quits at midnight. Haley stayed up to watch Christmas Vacation with my dad, the two of them practically lip syncing the entire movie together.

She fits so perfectly in my family; it makes me want to confess a lot of things to her. None of which I will because she's never once expressed getting serious with me. We're exclusive, but not committed. If that even makes sense.

In the silent darkness, her cell goes off.

"Ugh, watch that be Jenna, drunk off her ass." Haley climbs over me, straddling my hips to get her phone from the low hanging shelf with the docking station. She looks at the screen, and her smile falls so fast it makes me tense. "Hello?"

"About time you answered me," a woman sneers on the other end of the line. "Your father and I were worried sick about you."

Haley practically curls in on herself, sliding off my body and tucking her legs up. "What are you talking about?"

"You think you're too good to come home for break, is that it?"

"What? No. Dad said to not bother, so I didn't."

"Sure. Blame your dad."

I feel sick hearing the way her mother treats her. Haley won't look at me, and I want to rip the phone out of her hands to spare her more abuse.

"Where are you?"

Haley's gaze flicks to mine for a fraction of a second before she looks down again. "With a friend."

"A boy?"

"Yes."

"College turned you into a slut then. Nice."

"Mom." Haley's voice sounds strong even though she's shaking. "Stop."

"I'm just trying to understand why you'd choose to go home with someone else and be with their family instead of coming home to yours."

Oh, I can think of a million reasons why. Too bad she didn't ask me.

"A flight home is too expensive," Haley says cautiously. "I couldn't afford it."

There's silence on the line.

"Well, can you afford to pay your portion of the electricity bill at least? Or do you want your parents to suffer and freeze?"

Haley licks her lips. "No. I'll pay it. I'll…" She climbs off the bed and starts pacing. "I'll wire dad some more money."

"Don't bother. Send us cash."

"I can just pay it online."

"Why? Don't you trust me to pay with cash?" her mother huffs. "You're unbelievable, Haley. So hurtful. After all we've done for you, this is how you act? College has made you a snobby little bitch."

"Mom." Anger laces her voice, but so does hurt.

Enough of this bullshit. I snag the phone from her and say, "Hi Mrs. Davis. It's Cole."

"Oh!" Her tone changes completely. "Hi, Cole.

189

Happy Thanksgiving."

It takes everything in me to not tell her to shove a turkey leg up her ass. "Have a good night." I hang up and turn the cell off.

Haley cups her mouth as she stares at me, wide-eyed. "I can't believe you just hung up on her."

"I can't believe you didn't." Shit, I shouldn't have said that. Everyone handles their parents differently and clearly Haley's piece of shit family walks all over her. "Your mom is an asshole."

A little laugh bubbles out of her. "That's being too kind." She nestles against my arms, tucking in tight to me. "I'm sure she's having an aneurysm right now."

Does it make me a bad person to hope that's true? "You don't deserve to be treated like that, Hales."

She's quiet against me.

"As long as I'm here, I'm not going to let anyone disrespect you, Angel."

Her arm curls tighter around my middle. "Thank you," she whispers. "But I think I need to learn how to do this for myself. You aren't always going to be able to stick up for me."

My heart drops. "I could be," I say cautiously. "If you wanted me to be."

It's the closest I've come to telling Haley I love her. I don't know why I can't seem to get the words out yet.

"No." She then gives me the exact reason I keep holding back on telling her how I feel. "You have big things going for you, Cole. I'm not about to be the baggage that weighs you down."

"You're not baggage, Haley."

She doesn't say anything for a minute. We hold each other in the dark and I start questioning all my life choices because when I have her in my arms like this, nothing else matters.

"I'd give anything to have what you have, Cole." She runs her fingertips along my pecs. "Your parents love you so much. Your whole ass family is perfection."

"No family's perfect," I shoot back. "But yeah, mine's pretty great." I roll her over so she's straddling me again. "You want in on it?"

"Into your family?"

"Yeah, we're adopting you. You're in."

Haley giggles. "Wow. So soon?"

"Had to wait on the paperwork," I joke. "Didn't want to say anything before the final process was complete."

"Ah." She nods playfully. "And now it's all good? I'm in for sure?"

"Yeah, Angel. You're in." I run my hands up and down her back. "But just so you know, once you're in you can't back out."

Haley cracks a laugh. "Kinda like the mafia?"

"Pretty much."

She leans down and kisses me…

When I climb out of the memory, we're already back at the house. Shit, we've made the entire loop on one of my dad's many trails, and I have no idea how it happened. But when I look at Haley again, I see her differently than before.

"We should probably get going. It's a long

drive back."

"Okay," Haley's voice sounds hollow, defeated.

I can't fix that here, which is why I'm taking her home.

Chapter 21

Haley

When we make it back to my place, it's past midnight, but I'm not tired. I'm *drained*.

We didn't talk much on the way here. I can't shut my brain off. I've ruined Cole's holiday with my past hangups once again haunting me. Guilt eats me even as he laces our hands together and leads the way up to my apartment like nothing's wrong. My head and heart brace themselves for a fallout. I'm scared that I've taken two steps forward and three steps back with myself... and with him.

"I'm so sorry," I say while unlocking my door.

"You don't have anything to apologize for, Angel."

Opening things up, I kick off my shoes and drop my purse on the floor like it's a sack of trash. "I feel like I've ruined your night."

"You didn't." He toes his shoes off and lines them up by the door. When he walks towards me, he's predatory. Confident. Sexy as hell. "I want you to do something for me."

"Anything." I mean it. I'll do anything for this man. Besides, he still has a few days of free-use playtime with me, and he barely took advantage of it today. The prospect of picking up where we left off with that almost chases my blues away.

I think our love language is physical affection, only Cole gets cuddly and clingy while I just want him to rail me until I can reset my factory settings.

"Stand over by your bookshelf, facing it."

Umm. Okay. That's not what I thought he was going to say. So much for hoping we're going to screw each other's brains out so I can factory reset myself.

When I reach the bookshelf, I swear my pussy dries right up. It's nothing but a glorious display of how fucked in the head I've always been. How much effort I've had to put into carving a new life for myself that doesn't involve my toxic parents. I want to curl into a ball and cry about it. It's embarrassing to have grown up the way I did. And it's double awful that Cole knows so much about my past.

Does he look down on me for it?

Does he pity me?

"Stay just like you are," Cole growls from the couch. My back is to him, so I have no idea what he's doing. But when I feel him approach, my stomach flutters. "Daddy's so fucking proud of you, Angel." His hands glide down my arms and he grabs my wrists, placing my hands on the bookshelf. "Look at what a good job you've done."

I don't understand. "I haven't done anything."

Cole lifts my dress up to my hips. Then his hand lands hard on my bare ass. *Smack*! "Wanna try that again?"

Holy shit. What's happening here? "I..."

I'm so confused.

"Look at what a good job you've done," he growls against my ear. *Smack!* "Who's been such a good girl?" *Smack*! "Who knows her motherfucking worth now?" *Smack*!

My ass is on *fire*.

"I..." I can't breathe.

He spanks my ass again. "Say it." His breaths grow heavier. "Who's a good girl and knows her worth?"

"M-m-me?"

He spanks me again. "Is that a question or an answer, Angel?" He spanks me again before I can answer.

There's no relenting with him. The delicious pain makes my head spin. "Cole."

"Look at your hard work, Angel." He spanks me again. "Who's been a good girl?" *Smack*! "Working on herself so she doesn't ever let someone disrespect her again?" *Smack*!

Each strike burns hotter than the last.

And it all goes straight to my pussy.

"Me," I groan, tears pricking my eyes.

"That's right, Angel." He spanks me again. My ass jiggles and stings with each hit. I fucking love it. "Read your notes out loud for Daddy." *Smack*! My grip tightens on the bookcase because holy shit, this is going to make me come. "Do it."

Smack!

My gaze lands on the first bright note. "You're not a hindrance just being in someone's life."

"Keep going." *Smack*!

"You're a human, not baggage."

"That's my good girl." He spanks me again, then rubs my ass cheeks to soothe the burn. "More. Read more to me, Angel."

I glance at a green note, my vision a little blurry. "No one can make you feel worthless without your consent."

"That's right." He spanks me again. "That's my good fucking girl. Give me more."

My chest tightens. "Love yourself how you want others to love you."

Smack! "That's it." His breath skates down my neck, making my nipples harden even more. "Do you know how proud I am of you?" My heart flutters in my throat when he kicks my legs wide and presses his hot cock against my entrance. "You're gonna come so fucking hard for me tonight, Angel." He shoves his way inside me, stretching me, filling me. "Tell me what a good girl you are."

"I'm a good girl."

"That's right." His hips slam against me with each thrust. "Say it again."

"I'm…" Fuck, he's deep. "I'm a good girl."

"Yeah, you are." He winds my hair around his hand and tugs it. "Tell me more."

I'm not sure what he wants to hear.

Cole lets go of my hair and gives me a hand necklace instead. His thrusts are slow and deep, making me feel so full. "Tell me no one gets to disrespect you."

"No one gets…" He slams into me harder, and I pitch forward. "No one gets to disrespect me."

"You're worth waiting for."

My lungs are robbed of air with his next thrust. I'm on my tippy toes to accommodate his size, and the little purchase I have on the bookcase is slipping. Thankfully, it's bolted to the wall.

He pulls me flush against him and rocks his hips while holding my neck with one hand, the other has found my clit. "Say it and I'll let you come, Angel."

"I'm worth waiting for."

"Say it like you *fucking mean it*." He shoves me forward and slams into me harder.

"I'm worth waiting for."

"Louder." *Slam, slam, slam*. His hips turn into pistons as he rails me.

"I'm… worth…. waiting for."

"Fuck right, you are." He pulls out and spins me around. "Who is Daddy's Angel?" Cole lifts me up and impales me on his cock again. I feel dizzy as he slams me against the wall next to the shelf. "Look at me and say it. Who's my Angel?"

"Me. It's me. It's always been me." Tears sail down my cheeks and I'm not even sure if they're from sadness, elation, or sheer confusion from the pleasure/pain combo he's delivering.

We turn into a frenzy of kisses, thrusts, and grunts.

"God dayem, Angel. You make me crave you all fucking day and night." We've made it to my bed. With my legs hooked over his shoulders, Cole scrambles my insides. "I love making you this desperate to come for me."

Desperate is an understatement. I think I'll go insane if I don't get a release soon. Every time I get close, he switches things up on me and I lose the traction we've made.

"Beg your Daddy."

"Please," I whimper. "Please let me come now."

"Only if I can taste it." He slows his thrusts and kisses the side of my calf. "Ask me to eat that perfect pussy for you." Cole rolls his hips, driving my lust higher.

"Will you please…" *Mmmm, that feels so good. What's he hitting in there?* "Can you please taste me? I want you to eat my pussy."

He pulls out and drops to his knees.

"Oh fuck." My back arches when Cole stuffs two fingers in my pussy and latches his mouth to my clit. He plays with me, edges me. It's not long before I'm so swollen and needy from him driving me to the edge of pleasure over and over again, that the slightest brush of his tongue makes me implode.

The force of my orgasm is unreal. My thighs shake as they clamp around his head. My voice breaks as I scream his name. My heart slams against my bones, breaking me apart.

Cole glides up my body and shoves his big dick into me again. I dig my nails into his shoulders, holding on for dear life.

"So wet and tight," he says against my mouth. "I want to fill this pretty pussy up with my cum."

"Please." I groan when he rotates his hips. "*Please*, Cole. I want to feel you come inside me."

He hovers over me, our gazes locked. "Beg again."

"I need your cum," I whimper. "Fill me. Stuff me with it. *Please*."

He crushes his mouth to mine and kisses me like I'm the only thing that gives him life. When he breaks the kiss, his speed and force become brutal. Cole fucks me clean across the bed and lifts my hips to get as deep as possible. "Take everything I give you."

Sweat drips down his temples as he thrusts

into me harder.

I nearly black out with how good the pain is. Stars burst in my vision. I feel so alive and powerful. So used and needed. *Wanted*.

Holding the back of his neck, I roll my hips to meet his with each thrust. "That's it, Daddy. Fill your Angel up. Make me take it all."

"Ffffuuuuck."

His cock jerks inside me. Cole grunts and groans, completely losing his rhythm. I feel like I'm floating as he comes hard and long inside me. When he pulls out, Cole curses under his breath and shoves two fingers into my pussy, plugging me up. "Hold me inside you."

My body obeys, muscles contracting around his fingers. When he finally pulls out, Cole shoves them into my mouth so I can suck them clean. My lower belly cramps, making me wince.

Cole doesn't miss it. "I was too rough."

"No." My voice is raspy. "Not at all."

"You'd tell me if I was, right?"

Probably not. "I like it rough."

"And I'll give it to you how you like it, but I also need to make sure I don't go too far."

"There's no such thing as too far with me, Cole."

His expression softens because he knows we're no longer talking about my sexual limits. "Didn't used to be that way."

"I know." Before I had boundaries and barriers and a lot of red tape around my heart.

"I'm not the same person anymore."

A smile slowly spreads across his face. "I love you more now than I did then."

His confession rolls off his tongue so easily, it makes my heart trip. "You... love me?"

Cole slides his arms under me and lifts me up. Carrying me to my bathroom, he cocks his brow. "Is that going to be a problem, Angel?"

"Only if you plan on stopping."

"Haley, I haven't stopped loving you since the day you walked into my life."

Chapter 22

Cole

It's been three days since I left Haley's apartment. I can't stop thinking about her. After telling her I love her, we took a hot shower together and crashed for the night.

She didn't say I love you back.

But honestly, she doesn't have to. Her actions speak louder than words. Haley turned her world upside down and crawled her way back to me. Everything she's been through, all the shit she's put up with, it made her a tough girl growing up and forged her into the incredible woman she is now.

I'm a lucky motherfucker.

Too bad I'm also fucked in the head about it.

Ever since I was a kid, I've had this irrational fear of all the good things in my life getting taken away. As if bragging about a good grade will cause me to fail the next test. Having pride in myself will force the hands of fate to rip the rug out from under me and destroy my career.

Hell, I remember when I was really little, I

was afraid that if I liked the color of my eyes too much, I'd go blind and never be able to see again. Yeah, like I already said, it's irrational.

Doesn't make it any less terrifying, though.

This fear makes me hold back in some things.

Even when I fell in love with Haley, I held my breath and didn't say a word about it back then. The possibility of the universe looking down at me and saying, "Hey, this dumb fuck is insanely happy and in love. Let's destroy it for him and knock his ass down a few pegs," was a recurring nightmare for months.

Ironic that I didn't have to profess my love to her for me to still get my heart shattered, right?

To this day, I have no clue why I'm always waiting for the other shoe to drop. It's not like I have some unresolved past trauma that's made me this way. My life is great. I can roll with the punches. I make adjustments as needed and don't let things keep me down.

But in my darkest hours, I'll admit I'm fake. I pretend to be okay even when I'm not. I act better than I feel. I've protected myself, my peace, my heart, and my pride by holding back who I really am and what I want out of this life. I put up with shit I shouldn't have to.

I put up with people I don't like. *My boss.*

I've let people slip through my fingers. *Haley.*

I keep my head down and work hard, so I

don't have to sit alone in my condo, wondering what I'm doing with my life and fearing I'll forever be alone. *Like my brother, Reid.*

And even though everything is going great right now, I can't shake the terror of knowing there's a possibility of something, or someone, wrecking it all.

It makes me overly protective.

And seriously paranoid.

Haley and I have rebuilt our relationship so fast, it might be what gets hit first. I don't think she'd ghost me again, but what if her parents come back and derail her hard work?

What if she falls out of love with me?

What if —

My cell vibrates in my back pocket.

The frenzied what ifs vaporize when I see who's calling. "Hey, Angel."

An immediate calmness pours over my head when she replies with a sexy, sultry, "Hey, Daddy."

We can go into heavy detail on why these honorifics work for both of us, but I'm not about to dissect what doesn't need to be pulled apart. Our dynamic is perfection for a bunch of reasons that are no one else's business.

"Where are you?" I glance at the clock on my wall. It's six-thirty already. Damn, today flew by. "I'll come meet you."

"What if I'm on my way to get a root canal?"

"I'll come hold your hand and give

support."

"What if I'm in the middle of a gynecologist appointment?"

"I'll still come hold your hand and give support."

"What if I'm getting a tattoo of your face on my ass?"

"Then I'll definitely come hold your hand and give support. It's better to be there in person, anyway. Wouldn't want them to make my nose too big or anything." Her giggle is music to my ears. Closing my laptop, I get up and grab my coat, eager to be with her. "You hungry?"

"Starving. Want to meet up for dinner?"

"Tell me when and where. I'll be there."

"Your place. Half hour." Haley starts her engine. "I have a surprise for you."

I hope it comes with stilettos.

Hanging up, I bolt from my office, and nearly trample poor Tamara on my way out.

"Hey, Cole, I need to talk with you."

"Tomorrow." I holler from the elevator. "Whatever it is, it can wait until tomorrow."

The door closes with her staring at me, slack jawed.

I make it home in pretty good time, considering rush hour. Shoving my door open, I stop in my tracks when I see Haley in a pair of red fuck me pumps, a white feathery tutu, and my collar. The leash attached to it hangs down her back, hitting her calves as she walks around what can only be described as the most pathetic Christmas tree I've ever seen in my life.

It's three-foot tall, crooked, pre-lit...

And pink.

"What's this?" I stalk closer.

Haley turns and now I see she's got peppermint candy nipple clamps on her tits.

Holy. Shit.

"What's it look like?" She saunters over and kisses me. "I got us a Christmas tree."

Did I mention she's wearing a headband that has candy canes attached to little springs that make them bounce all over the place?

"Well." She purses her lips. "I didn't get us this Christmas tree. I already had it."

My chest tightens. I remember when she once told me she never had a Christmas tree growing up. Her parents couldn't afford one or didn't have a place to put one up. "This is yours?" I reach out and grab the wiry tip of a branch. It's all plastic.

"Yup! I got it on clearance at the end of the season three years ago. It's probably the first real thing I did to make a tradition for myself."

Scratch that. This is the best Christmas tree in the whole wide world.

I kiss her head, torn between appreciating the tree and the view of her decorating it in that outfit. "What's it doing in my house, Angel?"

"It brings me joy." She grins, staring at it. "I thought it might bring you joy, too."

"I love it." Standing behind her, I wrap my arms around her waist and kiss the back of her shoulder. "It's an amazing surprise."

"Oh, that's not the surprise." She wiggles away from me and plucks a box up from under the tree. "This is."

Arching my brow, I take it from her. "Do I open it now?"

"Mmm hmm."

It's really fucking hard to not stare at her. She's hot dressed like a sexy candy cane. And those nipple clamps? Fuuuuck. I want to lick every inch of her.

"Focus, Cole." She taps the box.

Oh. Right. The present.

Unwrapping the box, I pull out a new mask. It's heavier than what I'm used to wearing, but the details are insane. It's a skull with gears and metal bolts all over it.

With a knowing glance, I pull off my shirt and slip it over my head.

Haley's pupils blow wide like a cat with catnip. "Holy hell, I was not prepared."

Instead of talking, I tip my head to the side and study her. Then I hold my pointer finger up and rotate it, silently telling my girl to spin around.

She backs up and gives me a three-sixty that makes my dick hard as steel. "I went with candy canes because I figured they're sweet and twisted like me."

After grabbing her leash, I snap my fingers and point to the ground. She goes down on her knees automatically.

Such a good girl.

The way she looks up at me with those big blue eyes and pouty little mouth, it's no mystery why I call her Angel. She isn't here to save my soul. She's come to fucking snatch it.

"I want your dick in my mouth." Haley pulls on my belt, unfastening it in no time. Slipping my cock out, she pumps it a few times before licking the tip. "I've been thinking about it all day."

My chest rises and falls with each breath, and it's a struggle to see straight. Christ, the way this woman gives head is dangerous. It'll make a man offer her the world and be willing to die at her feet for even an ounce of her precious love.

It's me. I'm that man.

Tipping my head back, reveling in the way her mouth is so hot around my dick, I can't help but wonder how we got here. We've fallen right back into a routine where we work hard, fuck hard, and fall asleep every night at either her place or mine. It's exhilarating. It's perfect.

Maybe even too good to be true.

My eyes roll back as she takes more of me down her throat. I rest a hand on the top of her head as I fuck her pretty mouth. Red lipstick rings my shaft halfway down. Her tits sway, those little nipple clamps pinching her hard buds, and I want to come all over them.

My mask holds a lot of heat, making it hard to breathe. Sweat builds on my brow. But I love it. With only a large cut out for my eyes, I'm concealed from reality. I'm not Cole. She's not Haley.

I'm a stranger face-fucking a candy cane imp.

Fuck, she feels good. "I want to blow my load on your tits."

She looks up at me, her lashes clumping together, eyes watery from how hard I'm thrusting. Sweet, delicious gurgle noises fill my ears. "Hold them up for me, Angel."

I pull out of her mouth and pump my dick hard and fast. Jets of cum spurt out of me, painting her tits white. Her mouth hangs open, tongue out, and I shove back into it after my release is over. "Suck."

My tip is so sensitive it's almost too much to handle as she gives it all her attention. "That's my good girl."

Ripping the mask off, I inhale cool air and slowly pump between her swollen, red lips. I hold the sides of her head, rocking back and forth until my dick hardens again.

"Ready for Daddy's cock to fuck your pussy?"

Haley nods and groans.

I pull out. "Get on your hands and knees. Put that ass up for me."

Wrapping my hand around the leash attached to her neck, I give it a little pull. "You're such a beautiful bitch in heat."

Haley's back and shoulders drop as she melts. "Only for you. I go all day desperate for you to come home to me. To take me and use me."

Before giving her my cock again, I spread her ass cheeks and rim her tight hole. She makes a sound that encourages me to do it again. "I want to fuck this ass."

She looks over her shoulder at me, eyes wide, brows pinched. "How bad do you want it?"

Bad enough to beg. "I want to play with it first and put a plug in it." Otherwise, I might hurt her without meaning to. "Stay."

I quickly fish out the new toys I bought last week that I'd planned to save for Christmas. So much for that idea. Plucking a smaller butt plug out of its box, I prep it and pour extra lube on her ass. There's a hot pink jewel on the end, which I bet will look spectacular between her cheeks.

"Give me that ass, Angel."

She puckers the tight hole on purpose just to taunt me.

The act earns her two smacks, one on each cheek. My handprints bloom a bright red on her sweet skin.

"Do it again," I dare her. But she's too busy groaning against the sensation of the plug pushing in. I twist it around, probing her a little at a time until her body opens up and takes what

I give it. "So fucking pretty."

I slap her ass again.

Haley's face down on the floor, wiggling her ass at me. "Fuck me, Cole." She reaches between her legs and plays with herself. "I need this hole filled badly."

"Did I say you could play with yourself?"

She stops and puts her hand back up by her head on the floor.

"That's what I thought." I slap her ass again, so she learns her lesson. "Dirty girl thinks she can call the shots here, huh?" Angling my dick to her entrance, I shove inside her with one long, hard thrust and give her zero time to adjust. Her pussy's a tight fit, and with that plug in her ass, I bet she's having a hard time taking it all.

But she does anyway.

"You're doing so good for me, Angel." I pump in and out of her slowly, my hand winding around her leash again.

I've never seen a sexier thing in my life. Red, marked up ass. Jewel glinting. Pussy wrapped around my big dick. Collar fastened. Leash hooked.

She's all mine, and that's how she's fucking staying.

"Who do you belong to, Angel?"

"You." Her breath catches when I bottom out. "You, Daddy."

"That's right. And I take care of what's mine, don't I?"

"Y-yes."

Her thighs shake when I fuck her a little harder.

"Does my dirty little cock slut want to get off?"

"Yes," she rasps.

I yank on the leash until she has no other choice but to lift onto her knees. Then I growl into her ear, *"Beg harder."*

Chapter 23

Haley

I've never been so turned on in my life.

My ass is plugged. My pussy is full. My tits are sticky with his cum. My thighs won't stop shaking. My entire body is a live wire.

I'm so desperate, I can barely hold myself together. It's overwhelming. And the clamps on my nipples bring me just enough pain to drive me insane with pleasure, too.

I did this to myself.

I teased, taunted, and went overboard tonight for Cole. And the price is my sanity.

"Please," I scream-beg. "Please let me come, Daddy."

Cole positions me on his lap and reaches around my waist. Suddenly, there's an intense vibration against my clit.

Straddling him in reverse cowgirl, with my thighs spread wide, the collar around my neck pulled tight enough for me to work for each breath, I grow dizzy with lust. And that vibrator sends me right over the edge.

Coming hard enough to skip my next life, I

scream, cry, shake, and convulse against Cole. I squirt all over his floor. "What's happening?" I yell, unable to control it.

"That's a good girl. You're taking it so well, Angel. Keep going." He holds the vibrator against my swollen clit and won't let up even after I try to smack it away. It's too much. Everything's too much. "Give me more, Angel."

"I can't." My lungs saw, working overtime to get air into my system. "I can't take anymore."

"Yes, you can. Be my good girl and make that pussy squeeze my cock while you come again."

Well, when he puts it that way…

The desire to please Cole overrides everything else until I'm gyrating against the cock in my cunt, which pushes the plug in my ass, and moves the vibrator pressed to my clit. A fresh orgasm builds quickly, and I dig my nails into his thighs, bracing for another onslaught of pleasure.

"Oh God," I moan, just before another orgasm hits. My eyes roll back. I'm so dizzy I can't think.

A few seconds later, Cole catches his release. I'm so full, so sensitive, I can feel his dick throb inside me as he comes.

Gathering my hair, he sweeps it over my shoulder and gently kisses my neck while we both come down from our highs. "You okay?"

"Never better." My voice sounds far away and slurry. Lifting off his lap, I pitch forward, too exhausted to even hold myself up. "Take it out, Daddy."

He playfully twists the butt plug a couple of times, which only makes me melt more into the floorboards.

Cole pulls the plug out and the void is real. No more dick. No more toy. No more fun.

I feel hollow. Tears prick my eyes.

"Come here." He carries me to the bathroom. I think I've turned into a noodle.

"These nipple things hurt," I whisper, too tired to even take them off. "Help me?"

He rests me on the sink and takes off my clamps. Blood rushes to my hard buds and I'm fucking dying. Mouth open, my scream doesn't even come because I've lost all air in my lungs again. Holy smokes, that's intense.

Cole suckles one in his mouth, ever so gently, and then moves to the other. He takes his time giving me all the aftercare I need and cleans us both up. A couple hours later, I'm on the couch, under a bunch of blankets, while he orders us dinner.

My little candy cane headband lays bent on the floor beside my pink Christmas tree.

Cole sits next to me. "Food will be here in twenty."

He had to wipe down the floor where I'd squirted. "I can't believe I made such a big mess like that."

"Not gonna lie. That was impressive." He

slides me onto his lap. Cole is always getting his hands on me one way or another—lacing our fingers together, hugging, hooking his arm around my shoulder, sitting me on his lap. I never got affection growing up, so it took a lot of getting used to when Cole and I first hooked up.

It's not that I didn't like it. It was just different, I guess. But after a month of him constantly touching me, I was addicted. If he didn't touch, hug, or hold me, I'd think he was mad at me for something and would worry about what I did wrong. It was something else I had to work through.

Lately, however, I'm just as touchy-feely. Leaning back against his chest, I run my nails up and down his forearm. "When did you get all those new toys?"

"Last week." He rests his chin on my shoulder. "I was going to wait until Christmas to give them to you."

Speaking of… "I have another surprise for you."

Cole's chuckle rumbles against me. "If it's you in another outfit like that candy cane one, give me a minute to prepare myself. You got no business looking that fine in a headband and anal plug, Angel."

"Thanks." Knowing I turn Cole on is a big deal to me. "But it's not an outfit." Climbing off his lap, I ignore his fake pout and go over to the pink Christmas tree and grab the little bag I stashed behind it. "I didn't get a chance to wrap it, but…" I sit down next to him. "Close your eyes."

He gives me a "what are you up to now" look before shutting his peepers.

"Hold out your hand." I place the gift in his palm. "Okay, you can look now."

His brow furrows. "What the hell is this?"

"Hear me out." Excited, I get up on my knees and face him. "It's our new tradition."

Cole stares at the ugly ornament again.

"Every year, we're going to find the ugliest, tackiest ornament we can find." I point at my tree. "And hang it on that thing."

He leans back. "Every year?"

"Until we die." I hope he understands that this is, yet again, another gesture of my love. Another promise that I'm here to stay. "Do you love it?"

Cole stares at the blobfish made of blown glass, then drags his gaze back to me. His expression softens. "Yeah, I love it, Haley."

He goes over and hangs the ornament on the tree. Then backs away, staring at it. "I think that thing's going to give me nightmares."

"Imagine what the whole tree will look like in a decade. Our kids will be traumatized."

We both start laughing, then he realizes what I just said and sobers quickly.

"Kids, huh?" Cole sits back down next to me.

I shrug. "Maybe?" We're nowhere near that topic of conversation in our relationship yet, but might as well put it out there for the future. "I remember you saying you want a bunch."

He doesn't look at me. "Yeah, I did."

"*Did*... as in you don't now?" My heart deflates a little.

"I'm not sure what I want," he says quietly.

"Oh." My stomach drops.

Cole tips my chin, forcing me to look at him. "But I know whatever it is, I want it with you."

Tears fill my eyes and I blink them back. "I've either sprung a leak or I'm getting soft." I widen my eyes so the tears don't fall and push away the embarrassment of looking vulnerable and scared of rejection. "Get back, feelings. Stay on the inside."

"It's okay to show your emotions, Haley. I promise it won't hurt you."

I know he didn't mean for it to happen, but his words hit like a crowbar. My feelings used to give my parents power over me. If they sensed a weak link in my armor, they'd pound on it until I caved and did whatever they wanted. Felt how they wanted me to feel. Said whatever they wanted me to say.

Cole's the opposite. He sees my feelings as another way to support me. Lift me. Care for me.

"I know my feelings are safe with you." Lacing my fingers with his, I lean back on the couch. "And you can celebrate your achievements and tell others about them, Mr. Architect. The other shoe won't always drop. I promise."

"Damn. You just had to call me out on that, huh?" Cole laughs. "Touché."

Our food arrives, and while I grab it from the delivery guy, he makes a call.

"Hey, Dad. Guess what?"

Joy fills my heart as Cole tells his father about the Marine Life building, and the pride that erupts from the other end of the line is so loud that I can hear it from across the room.

Cole's smile is huge. He runs a hand over his head, leaning back on the couch with his legs spread, and looks over at me. "Thanks, Dad."

I try to keep quiet while plating our cheesesteaks in the kitchen. When Cole hangs up, I saunter over and hand him a plate. "Good job."

He cocks a brow at me, his gaze slowly gliding up and down my body. "What's my reward?"

"Clean your plate and I'll give you dessert."

"I fucking love you."

"I love you, too."

Always have. Always will.

As far as second chances go, ours is turning out pretty epic.

Later that night, I fall asleep in Cole's arms, fantasizing about our future.

And praying nothing will fuck it up.

Chapter 24

Cole

Two weeks later...

I can't wait to see what Haley's pulled together for tonight's company party. And knowing the people on the invitation list? Well, if she knocks this out of the stratosphere, like I know damn well she will, Haley will have events booked out for the next five years.

I can't wait to watch my girl soar.

These past two weeks have been a dream and I'm counting all my motherfucking blessings.

Grabbing a decent parking spot in the lot, I see Haley's beat-up car in the corner, under a bright light. I know she got here early to set up, but I hope she still found time to eat something today.

Heading into the Gantz Plaza, I'm eager to see my girl.

A woman in a black pantsuit greets me immediately. "Good evening, sir. Are you here for the NGC Architects event?"

"Yes." My gaze sails around the lobby,

looking for Haley.

"You're a little early," she says, like she's not about to let me in. "We're still setting up."

"I'm here for Haley, actually."

"Oh!" Her eyes round. "I'll take you to her."

The front of the lobby only has a reception desk and small sitting area. This place used to be a cannery, which turned into an art gallery, and now it's a quirky place that focuses mostly on weddings and conferences.

The woman opens a set of double doors and I'm suddenly awestruck.

Holy. Shit.

It's like I just stepped into a fantasy realm. Swaths of fabric, green garland, and white lights drape across the ceiling, giving the huge, cold space a cozier feel. The tables are covered in snow white cloth with pinecone laden evergreens running along the center. Instead of typical circular tables, they're rectangular and each chair has dried oranges and evergreens with silver balls hanging off the back. Candelabras stretch across the tables, along with these crazy looking white flower arrangements. I smell rosemary and cloves, too.

"Put those over by the bar, please," I hear Haley say.

She's hunched over a table in the corner with her back to me.

"Thanks," I whisper to the woman who escorted me in. "I see her."

What an understatement. Haley's all I see. She's in a winter white cocktail dress and a pair of slippers. Her hair's pulled back in a low ponytail.

I sneak up behind her and tug her hair.

She turns around with a mean mug that quickly shifts to absolute joy. "Damn, Cole." She steps back and gives me an exaggerated up and down look. "You look amazing."

"So do you." I point at her slippers. "Nice touch."

"I can't wear my fancy shoes all day. I'd die. I only put the dress on a half hour ago, then got right back to adding the final touches to the room." She sweeps her arm out. "What do you think?"

"Amazing," I say, grinning. We both know I'm not talking about the room. "Stunning."

She giggles and slaps my arm. I notice her cell phone is on the table with a timer going. "Does this place blow up in twenty minutes and…" I look at it again. "Sixteen seconds?"

"That's my get ready timer. I have until the alarm chimes to get all the final details in order and then I disappear behind the curtain with a half hour to spare before guests arrive."

"Haley, what would you like us to do with the podium?"

She turns to the young man dressed in black pants and a button-down. "Can you put it to the side, over there? And check the mic for me, please?"

"No problem."

Her eyes suddenly widen with panic. "The high-tops!" Haley rushes towards the lobby. "Alyssa, are the high-tops set up in the other room yet?" She doesn't wait for an answer. My girl marches in and I follow. "Oh, phew."

This room is much smaller but has two bars set up with more garland everywhere, and several high-top tables. The caterer is setting out the charcuterie stations. Haley looks around, her lips in a tight thin line, as she assesses the room. "I still need those lights turned on," she announces. Then she picks up a huge, gilded frame that says, *"NGC Architects thanks you for your support and hard work. May the new year bring much joy to each of you!"*

Noah is going to love it.

He wouldn't think of thanking his clients and employees, but he'll damn sure take the credit for the gesture.

Haley scurries around and turns on all these little battery-operated lights in glass cylinders filled with more wintery decorations. This room is beautiful too, but it's not a showstopper like the main room is. I'm sure Haley's designed it that way on purpose.

Both rooms are elegant, classy, and cozy without being ostentatious.

"I went for a more casual feel in this room. It's better for icebreakers and warming up into conversations." She points at the bar. "There's also three signature drinks this evening."

My girl has thought of everything.

She escorts me over to the bar where a man's setting out napkins. "What can I get you, sir?"

Hmmm. I don't normally drink at these things, but tonight's a good night to celebrate. Scanning the framed menu, I gawk at the signature cocktails.

Cranberry Mule, Mistletoe Martini, and the Cole Crush.

"What do you think of the menu?"

Shit, shit, shit. "Very cute." I don't have the heart to tell her she spelled *coal* wrong.

"It's not a mistake," she says with a wicked little grin, as if she can read my mind. "Cole is spelled correctly. It's why the name is in a different color than the rest, too."

What the —

"Can he get the Cole Crush, please? Thanks." Haley's smile is all kinds of adorably wicked when she looks up at me.

The bartender places a milky white drink with a candy cane rim in front of us. "Enjoy."

I'm still stunned. "You named a drink after *me*?"

"Hey, I'm still celebrating your success. And since I'm the one in charge of this crazy operation, I get to do what I want." She tilts her head and puts her hands on her hips. "How's it taste?"

I take a little sip. It's smooth, and the mint isn't overpowering at all. I think there's white chocolate in it too. "Delicious."

She winks and walks away from me to get back to work.

I snatch her arm before she gets too far from me and kiss her hard. When we draw back, I love that I've smeared her lipstick. Dragging my thumb across the bottom of her lip, I fix it and say, "I'm really proud of you, Haley."

Her cheeks turn pink and eyes get a little glassy. My girl still doesn't know how to handle compliments. Especially when they come from people she cares about. And the fact that she's getting emotional over a single crumb of praise speaks volumes for her growth. At least it does to me. I'm glad she shows me her vulnerabilities. I love that she trusts me with them.

"Thank you." Haley gives me another peck on the mouth. "Now if you don't mind, I have to switch my shoes, fix my hair, and get ready to make NGC have the best party ever."

I smack her ass as she leaves me and smile behind the tumbler filled with liquid courage. Tonight's going to be amazing. The place is stunning, everything's in order, guests are going to roll in any minute, and I'm on cloud nine.

Nothing can possibly go wrong.

Chapter 25

Haley

I'm killing it.

Slipping through the crowd, making sure everything is going smoothly, and no one needs anything special, I get to hear all the things people are saying about my creativity.

I know this is Cole's night. Or more specifically, his company's big night, but it's mine too. If I can impress these people, maybe they'll keep me in mind for the future. Event planning isn't an easy business to get into. Especially in this economy. Good thing I'm really crafty and frugal. Even with this party, I was able to cut a lot of corners and use things that look expensive but were dirt cheap.

Honestly, it's probably all thanks to my parents that I'm like this. I can make a trash meal look gourmet if I want to.

Ugh, my parents. Even though I have zero regrets about cutting them out of my life, I still think about them. Still worry about them.

And lately, with Cole always hyping me up and telling me how proud he is of what I've accomplished, it's hit hard that I'll never hear that from my mom and dad. I'm so glad Cole's parents are better than mine. Hearing his dad whoop and holler on the phone when Cole told him about the Marine Life building definitely patched a hole in my heart that my upbringing made.

To celebrate my man's accomplishments is as wonderful as celebrating my own. It's not just exhilarating, it's healing.

The caterers bustle around, serving appetizers and snatching empty glasses. The signature cocktails are a hit. I'm thrilled. Standing in the corner, monitoring everything, I'm floating with the adrenaline that always hits me when I throw a party.

Cole cracks a boisterous laugh from one of the high-tops.

Aww, he's so happy.

When I packed my life up and moved to Banner Bay, I never would have guessed our reunion would happen so fast and effortlessly. I owe it all to Cole saying we could start with a clean slate. He meant it and I will forever be grateful he gave us a second chance.

"You're Haley, right?" a curvy, sexy brunette asks. There's a mistletoe martini in her hand.

"Yes. Hi." I hold out my hand for her to shake.

"I'm Tamara. Noah's assistant."

"Oh my gosh, *Hi*," I say again, this time with

a lot more gusto. "Cole's told me so much about you." She's his work wife and I love that for her.

"This place looks amazing." Tamara's gaze glides around the room. "Cole's hyping you up big time, too. I think it's his mission to have everyone here use you for every occasion."

Noooo. This isn't about me, it's *his* night! Why's he hyping me up when he should be hyping himself up? "He's so sweet."

Jaedyn saunters over, one hand in his pocket. "Haley, it's so nice to see you again."

"You too, Jaedyn." I shake his hand. "Enjoying cocktail hour?"

"These drinks are stupid good." He takes a healthy sip of his Cranberry Mule. "Tamara, Noah's asking for you."

She rolls her eyes and sighs. "Okay." She flashes me a smile and then quickly leaves with Jaedyn at her side.

It doesn't take a rocket scientist to know they're a couple. Not with how Jaedyn's been staring at her all night.

The head of Blue House Catering rushes over. "We're going to sound the bell in three minutes," she says.

"Perfect."

When the bell sounds and everyone moves into the larger room, I hold back my smile when I hear them *oooh* and *ahhh* over the way the room looks.

"I want the name of their coordinator,"

someone says. "They've got to do my daughter's wedding."

"I wonder where Noah found them?" someone else says. "I'll have to ask for their contact information."

"Next Level Events," Cole says, hearing them talk. "Her name's Haley Davis and she's incredible. I'll send you her contact number if you'd like."

"You're a saint, Cole. Thank you." The woman rests her hand on his arm as they enter the room together. "Oh my heavens, look at this place."

He looks back at me and winks.

• • •

Cole

"And then I said, get me a corn dog, and everyone laughed." Noah leans forward in his chair, clearly intoxicated.

I look around and flag down a server. "Can we get some more water?"

"Sure thing." He scurries off to grab a pitcher.

Noah has a speech to make soon, and he's already shitfaced. Seriously? This fucker is so unprofessional sometimes.

"It was *hilarious*!" He laughs obnoxiously. "You had to be there."

"Clearly," Charles Bowman says, dryly. "So, Cole." He turns his attention to me. "We're really excited to work with you on our marine life protection effort."

"I'm thrilled to have the honor, sir. Ocean conservation is so important."

"It truly is. My daughter is a marine biologist. She's been working closely with several environmentalists in this area, and all along the East and West Coasts, to set up facilities that can hopefully help the environment."

"That's amazing." I'm genuinely intrigued. "So does she want to focus more on animals or corals?"

"Both." Charles smiles. "I think if she had her way, there would be frag nurseries along the entire shoreline of the U.S., Indonesia, and Australia."

"What a dream." I take a sip of my ice water. "It'll be an honor to work with you both to make it come true, Sir."

"Please, call me Charlie. We're going to be working closely for the next three years or so to get your design up, and being called anything else makes me feel old."

Across from me, Noah's going on and on about something to Charlie's wife, Sinclair. She doesn't seem happy and worry creeps into my system. As she takes a sip of her wine, she looks over at Charlie and arches her brow.

It's a signal for help.

Fuck.

"Come on, baby," Noah mumbles, all up in her personal space. "Go for a ride with me."

Sinclair's eyes widen and she stands. "Charlie. We're leaving."

Shit. Shit. SHIT!

Just as Charlie asks her, "What's wrong?", Haley taps Noah's shoulder and there's a microphone in her hand.

Dread consumes me.

"It's time for your speech," Haley says, smiling.

"Right." Noah shoves out of his seat and stumbles away from the table.

Charlie stands up with Sinclair mirroring him. "Unbelievable."

I can barely keep up with the number of things going wrong at once. "How about I take it?" I say, jumping into action.

"No, I've got it." Noah sways, and I hold his arm to keep him steady.

"You're wasted," I whisper against his ear. "Please, Noah, let me handle this." I've never seen him this shitfaced before. I really didn't even see him drink that much, to be honest.

"I said I've got it." He shoves me back. "This is *my* company. It's *my* speech. It's *my* party."

He's making a scene.

"Tamara," he hollers. "Where are my notes?"

Tamara pushes out of her chair and rushes

over. "You didn't give them to me, Noah." She looks over at me, her face paling with panic. "What's wrong with him?" she mouths to me.

I shrug.

"Never mind, here they are." He yanks his cell out of his pocket and a little baggie filled with white powder falls out with it.

Holy. Shit.

This cannot be happening.

This. Cannot. Be. Happening.

With the long tables, and everybody staring at us, more than a dozen people can plainly see the drugs on the floor by Noah's foot. He doesn't notice. And as he stumbles over to snatch the mic from Haley, something in me turns feral.

I don't want him near her.

I don't want him here, *period*.

Jaedyn and Avery are on Noah in a flash. "We got this," Jaedyn says, steering Noah away. Avery picks up the baggie from the floor and ducks his head, heading out after them. Numbly, I grab the mic and head to the center of the room.

My bowtie is strangling me.

The room's spinning a little.

"On behalf of..." *Fuck my life, I can't believe this is happening*. Clearing my throat, I try again. "On behalf of NGC Architects, I want to thank all of you for your support this year. We're a tight-knit family who spends a lot of hours working together, and during this time of year, it's good to appreciate what we've created together. I know

Noah is grateful for the team he's built and everyone who trusts NGC to design buildings that have turned Banner Bay into a beautiful, thriving area for so many." Charlie and Sinclair march towards the door and my heart falls out of my ass. "May the New Year be happy, successful, and filled with love for everyone. Thank you so much for coming tonight and being a part of NGC's extended family."

The applause sounds muffled in my ears as I hurry out the door to chase Charlie and Sinclair down. There's no way I can let them leave without apologizing to them first.

"Sir!" I yell, running through the lobby. But I stop dead in my tracks when I see him talking furiously with Jaedyn, who looks like he's just been kicked in the balls.

"We will not work with a company who is so disrespectful and disgusting. Tell Noah the deal is off."

I freeze in the middle of the lobby.

No.

NO!

Charlie doesn't even see me as he puts his arm protectively around his wife and escorts her out of the building.

Chapter 26

Haley

I find Cole sitting in the lobby with his face buried in his hands.

My heart drops.

"Cole?"

"Give me a minute." His voice is ragged and deep. His knee bobs fast and he looks like he's going to explode.

"Haley." The head of catering heads over to me. "Last call on the open bar, in case you want to let everyone know."

"Just break it down," I say. No need to make another announcement. My focus is only on Cole, fuck all else. Pulling up a chair, I sit with him and fold my hands in my lap.

We don't speak.

I don't even know what to say. I'm not even sure what happened that would make him this devastated, but the possibilities flying through my imagination aren't good.

"They pulled the deal," he says gruffly. "The Marine Life building. They pulled it because of Noah."

My heart breaks for him. "Cole, I'm so sorry."

"Don't apologize for shit you didn't do." He leans back and sighs. "I *knew* it was too good to be true. I *knew* I shouldn't have been this happy before we broke ground."

"This isn't your fault, Cole. You deserve that deal. You deserve to be happy." Hopping up, I look around, preparing to help him anyway I can. "I'm going to talk with them. It was the guy with the silver hair, right? With the woman in that purple gown?"

"Sit down, Haley." His voice is gruff. "They already left."

Damn. I drop back into the chair, at a loss for what to do.

He grabs my hand, squeezing it. "Thank you."

"I didn't do anything."

"You were going to. That's just as good." His hand is warm and heavy in mine. "You know the irony of this is, I was going to quit."

"What?"

Cole nods. "I had plans to quit at the start of the New Year. And that project made me toss those plans in the trash. I was willing to stay, to put up with Noah and his bullshit, because I wanted that success so fucking bad."

He can still have that success without Noah.

"I didn't know he had a drug problem." Cole stares at the carpet. "But now that I'm looking back, the signs were there. I just didn't notice them because I always kept my nose to the drafting board, busting my ass, hoping for my big break."

His knee won't stop bobbing.

"What are you going to do now?"

He runs his palms along his thighs. "I'm going home. If I stay here any longer, I'll beat that motherfucker to pulp, and I really don't want jail time."

"Okay." I wish I could go with him, but I don't think having me around will help. I know all too well that sometimes you need to handle shit by yourself. It's how I survived most of my life. But I want to be there with him through this pain. He shouldn't have to bear it alone. It's not fair.

He leans over and kisses my temple. "Bye, Angel."

I watch Cole sulk out the door, taking my heart and soul with him.

• • •

When I arrive at Cole's place, it's past midnight. The lights are out, and I don't know if I should leave or crawl into bed with him.

I'm completely out of my element.

All this time, we've been in sync, like a pair of newlyweds who can't keep their hands off each other. He gave me a key to his place, and he has one to mine. It's been easy. So easy.

Too easy.

But tonight, I feel like an intruder.

Toeing my shoes off, I creep through his condo and head for the bedroom. There's a faint glow of a laptop screen and he casually shuts it when I enter the room.

"Hey," I say quietly. "You okay?"

He doesn't answer as he sets his laptop on the floor and leans back on his pillows. The moonlight filters in from the windows, casting shadows across the bed.

Dread twists my gut. "Do you want to be alone?"

"No." His answer spreads through the darkness of his bedroom, landing square in my chest.

"Jaedyn and Tamara were able to—"

"I don't want to talk about any of them."

"Okay." Crawling onto the bed, I sit on my knees with my hands in my lap again. "Do you want to talk at all?"

"No." He sits up and cups my face. Pressing his mouth to mine, he kisses me slowly. Deeply.

I mean, talking can be overrated sometimes. And since I know physical touch is his love language, maybe this will help comfort more than my words can.

His hands drift down my back and he unzips my dress slowly. Peeling it off my shoulders, he shoves it down. "You look beautiful in white." Cole's fingers trace the curve of my breasts. "The moonlight hits you in all the best places."

I swallow the lump in my tightening throat. Straddling him with my dress bunched up around my waist, I kiss Cole again. This is different for us. Instead of being two clashing forces of nature tearing at each other, we're softer. Slower. More deliberate.

"Make love to me, Haley." His hands skate down my back. His dick is hard between my thighs, under the covers.

Cupping the back of his head, I kiss him softly and it's like the night we took each other's virginity.

We're tentative. Cautious. Caring.

"I love you," I say against his mouth. "Fuck, Cole, I love you so damn much."

He groans against my mouth.

With a little effort, we get my dress completely off and I hover over his bare cock. Our eyes lock as I sink down on him. My thighs shake. A breath shudders out of him. Every noise he makes turns me inside out. To know I feel so good to Cole that he can't help but make these sounds is a heady thing.

"You feel so good, Angel." He buries his hand in my hair, holding the back of my head while he kisses me again. We move together, our bodies undulating, heat rolling off us both. "Fuck me slowly," he says. "Keep your eyes on mine."

He holds my hips, moving me at the pace he wants. Our eyes remain deadlocked on each other, and I feel like time and space no longer exist.

Years of solitude, of yearning, of regrets and sorrow vaporize.

"That's it," he says in a low tone. "Just like that."

He's so deep inside me like this that when I swing my hips back and forth, grinding against him, I swear I feel it from my head to my toes. We lace our hands together and I use his strength as leverage. His hands shake in mine. His breaths quicken.

I'm so close to an orgasm, my rhythm falters. When it finally hits, I milk his cock, my inner walls clamping down hard as I come.

"*Haley.*" His abs flex and he groans loudly. "Don't stop." Cole sits up and rocks me back and forth. His orgasm rips out of him and his body shakes. We both collapse on the bed, me still on top, and he holds me tight. "Thank you."

What's he thanking me for? "I didn't do anything."

Cole swipes the hair from my face when I look up at him. "You came back."

He's not talking about tonight.

"I came *home.*"

It isn't always a shelter. Sometimes it's the love of your life.

Chapter 27

Cole

Quitting my dream job shouldn't have felt so freeing. I guess it's confirmation I did the right thing.

It was awkward as fuck when I rolled into the office, resignation letter out and signed. A companywide email saying my goodbyes was scheduled for the same time I slapped my resignation letter on Noah's desk.

He didn't have shit to say. Just stared at the letter and gritted his teeth.

"Get help," I growled at him. Then I turned away and packed my things.

I also made sure to have Haley's check in hand before I left the office for good. I wasn't sure if Noah would screw her over or not, but I wasn't taking the risk. My girl gave him more than he deserved, and he was going to pay accordingly.

"What are you going to do now?" Tamara had asked.

"I don't know yet," was my reply.

That was three weeks ago, and I still don't have a fucking answer.

Good news is, I didn't have a non-compete clause in my contract with NGC. Noah's mistake is my relief.

Double good news is, since I worked on Haley's office design on my own, and never had her sign a contract, she's still able to roll with the plans, free of charge, just like I'd planned.

I know enough construction companies, thanks to my work, my dad, and my brother Trey, that hiring a small crew to get her office up and running is easy.

Speaking of my girl, she's killing it. Haley's been up to her eyeballs with phone calls, people booking weddings in the area, and even up to two states away. She'd taken a video of the NGC night and posted it on social media. It got a decent number of views, but I'd talked her up to everyone with a set of ears, and she says that's what really helped.

Maybe I can make a living being Haley's personal hype man.

Talk about a dream job.

I'd brag about my Angel all day and night if I could.

Checking the time on my phone, I head down the street, pulling my beanie tighter on my head. It's cold as fuck out. I smell snow.

I'm meeting Haley at a coffee shop in town. Don't know why she wants to see me in the middle of the day like this, but I'm not complaining. Shit, any time my girl wants to see me, I'll be there.

Besides, I'm going stir crazy at home. Putting feelers out for another job has been frustrating as hell.

Holding the door for a lady in a red coat, I let her through first, then head in. Unzipping my coat, I scan the café for my girl.

She's not here yet.

Cool. Cool. I'll just order her favorite and wait.

I order two lattes and when I pick them up at the other end of the café, I run into someone I never thought I'd see again. My stomach plummets.

Charles Bowman.

"Cole." He grabs his coffee from the counter and gestures to a table with his coat already hanging off one chair. "Have a seat."

It takes a hot minute for my brain to make my body move correctly. I cautiously head over and sit down with him. "It's good to see you again."

Am I in the twilight zone? "You too, Sir."

"I'm going to cut to the chase," he says, pushing his coffee cup out of the way. "I heard you quit NGC."

My tongue feels fat in my mouth. Like a dipshit, I nod.

Charles taps the table. "I'm glad."

"It was overdue," I manage to say. "I only planned to stay when I got the deal with you.

Once that was gone, there was no reason to stick around."

He leans back in his chair with his arms crossed. "I couldn't in good conscience work with a company like that. Noah was incredibly out of line with my wife."

"I'm sorry you and Mrs. Bowman were disrespected."

"Don't apologize for things you didn't do. That's on Noah. Not you." He clears his throat. "And we only went with Noah because I'd seen some of your designs from colleagues of mine. I'm on a lot of boards, Cole. *A lot*. And I have a lot of fucking money."

My stomach clenches. I have no clue what he's trying to say to me.

"I'm always disappointed when my colleagues don't have the balls to step outside of conventional designs."

"Classics are classics for a reason, sir. They stand the test of time."

"True. But that's not how you make a statement. You can't pave a way to greatness by playing it safe. The future needs boldness. It needs leaders who aren't afraid to stand out."

I still have no clue where he's going with this.

Charles looks down at his hands. "My wife and daughter are meeting with Next Level Events right now, making wedding plans."

My heart swells with pride for Hales.

"They'll love working with Haley. She's incredibly talented and so genuine."

"And she's yours, right? You two are a couple?"

What the fuck?

"Yes, Sir. She's..." I look down, shaking my head and chuckling. "She's the love of my life. The only one I've ever had."

"I was the same way with Sinclair. She's the greatest thing that ever happened to me. I'll do anything for her. And also, my daughter."

"I get it."

His expression turns more serious. "A smart man knows when the right thing comes along and he better grab it with both hands and not let go."

"Yes, sir. No, sir." I'm not even sure how to correctly answer him.

"You're that right thing, Cole."

I'm so fucking confused.

He must see it on my face because he quickly adds, "I still want you to work with us. I didn't sign the contract with NGC so it's not under Noah's control. Fucking good timing on that one. My secretary went home sick the day I sent the email letting Noah know we'd chosen your design. When she came back to work, she was so overwhelmed with catching up, she never got the contract out. I ripped it up the day after the party."

My heart skitters around in my chest. *Talk about good timing.*

"I wasn't joking about putting up buildings all over the shorelines. I'm working with some big companies to secure property in seven major coastal sites." He tips his head. "I'd love for you to design each one for us."

Thank God I'm sitting down, or I'd fall flat on my ass.

"Are you serious?"

"I don't joke about money, Cole. And this is going to be a lot of money." He holds his hand out for me to shake. "What do you say? Want to change the world with me and potentially save a bunch of sea life at the same time?"

My palms are clammy. "Yes, sir." I shake his hand, feeling lightheaded. "Absolutely."

"I knew you were a smart man." He chuckles and leans back in his chair. Then his gaze drifts over my shoulder. "Ah. Here come our better halves."

I turn to see Haley and Sinclair enter the café, both laughing.

Haley's eyes meet mine, and her smile is so warm it makes me melt.

"I'll be in touch," Charlie says. "Haley gave my wife your number already."

With that, he leaves with Sinclair and Haley comes over, planting a big kiss on my cheek. "Hi."

"You are something else," I say, my mind reeling.

"By something else, you mean amazing,

smart, and built to fuck, then yeah, you're right." She grabs her drink from the table. "Are you happy?"

Her question has nothing to do with us, and everything to do with what just happened between me and Charles Bowman.

"He's hiring me to design conservation buildings all along the coasts. Seven, in fact."

The cup slips right out of Haley's hand and splashes all over the floor. She practically jumps into my lap. "I'm so fucking proud of you!"

"Thanks." I wrap my arms around her and squeeze. "I hear you're planning their daughter's wedding?"

"I am." She wiggles her ass in my lap. "And she's getting the royal treatment."

"As all brides should."

Haley's so excited, she's practically vibrating. "This is amazing. You're amazing. Everything's amazing."

It sure is.

Timing is everything. Things don't always happen when you want them to.

They happen when they're *meant* to.

And this? This is *our* time.

Epilogue

Cole

Two years later…

Haley: I want you.

I stare at the text and lick my lips. I lost a game of PIG over the weekend, and now my wife gets three free-use days out of me.

I said what I said.

Cole: On my way.

I pass the ugly pink Christmas tree that now has a few more hideous ornaments on it, and head out of our house that I designed myself. These past two years have been a whirlwind. Moving, marriage, the Marine Life projects.

What's next?

I can't wait to find out.

Making it to Haley's office in record time, I sprint to her floor. It's two in the afternoon, so I'm sure they're busy preparing table seating charts and shit.

My girl's business is booming. She's amazing. Everyone loves her.

And I'm the lucky sonofabitch who gets to

kiss her good morning and fuck her to sleep every night.

Her office is kitted out with all kinds of luxury. You don't come to her for a pizza party, you come to her for a million-dollar wedding. Although, she would totally throw a banging pizza party if you asked. She caters accordingly. No event too small, no wish list too big. But most of her clients have extremely deep pockets.

Her dream office looks exactly like the drawing she gave me two years ago. The pride I feel every time I come here never gets old. It's usually bustling with staff working on centerpieces and designs or meeting with clients. This afternoon is super quiet.

"Where is everyone?" I ask, entering Haley's big office. Her beautiful orchid has thirteen buds on it, all ready to burst into blooms.

"I gave them the rest of the day off." Haley swerves around in her chair. Naked. She props her feet on the desk and spreads her legs. "Get over here and lick my pussy."

"Yes. Ma'am."

Did I mention how much I love my life?

Usually, I'm the one who gets free-use of Haley, but having the tables turned for once is really fun. I didn't think I'd enjoy being her fucktoy as much as I do.

Oh, who am I kidding. Yes, I did.

I crawl under her desk and roll her chair back until it hits the big windowsill behind her.

"Put your feet on my shoulders."

She bites her lip and does what I say.

Her pussy is drenched already. "What have you been thinking about, bad girl?" I shove a finger into her and pump it.

"You. Always you." She reaches behind her and grabs something. When I look up, she's wearing a mask.

My mask. The one I wear that only has a window for your eyes.

Oh. Fuck.

This is new. I think I like it.

She snaps her fingers and points at her pussy.

I definitely like it.

I suck her clit and fingerbang her until she's clutching the armrests of her chair, screaming my name. She tears the mask off and pants.

"Thank me," she orders.

"Thank you, Angel."

"For what?"

"Feeding me." I lick her again, loving the way she melts on my tongue.

"Fuck me," she says next.

Haley starts ripping at my shirt while I take care of my pants. Turning her around, I press her hands to the window. "Spread your legs, Angel."

She lifts onto her toes, and I slam home in one thrust.

"You take this cock so well." I rail her hard while she gets a great view of the street. "Such a good." *Slam.* "Girl." *Slam.* "You needed Daddy's cock so bad, didn't you?"

"Yes," she grunts. "I couldn't wait another minute."

I bite her shoulder, kneading her tits hard like she loves and fuck her until she's a quivering mess. Tugging her hair, I rotate my hips and slam into her harder. "You're doing such a good job, Angel. Letting me use all your holes."

She's close to another orgasm.

Pulling out, I spin her around and lift her up, then impale her again. I fuck her on the desk, the chair, the wall, and we finally land on the large conference table. Haley grips the edge, holding on for dear life while I fuck her mercilessly.

"That's it, Angel. Come around my cock." Holding her with a nice hand necklace, I make her look at me. "Stay with me," I growl. "Stay right here. Look at me when you come, Angel."

She rubs her clit while I rearrange her insides and less than a minute later, she's screaming my name.

I unload at the same time she does, and we both sink into each other. My heart's beating a mile a minute.

Christ, I might stroke out.

We finally peel off each other to catch our breaths.

"Nice touch with the mask."

"Thought you'd appreciate it." Haley keeps

her legs wrapped around me. "I missed you all day today."

"Oh yeah?" I nip her bottom lip. "Me or this dick?"

"Is there a difference?" she teases.

I spank her ass for that one.

She makes another snarky comment, and I spank her ass two more times.

"Keep punishing me and I'll come again," she warns.

Quick as a whip, I bend her over and spank her until she's a writhing mess, clawing at the table. Her ass is a beautiful cherry red now.

She giggles, stumbling when she tries to stand again. "We need to play PIG again. I'm making it my life's mission to kick your ass every time so I can have more free-use days." Her hand sails down to play with her clit again.

"Greedy girl." I slap her hand away and sink to my knees so I can eat her until she comes again. Haley's insatiable. I think I've created a monster.

After I've made her come so much, she begs to me stop; I get her dressed and we head out for an early dinner.

"I have a surprise for you," she says, as we sit in our favorite booth at the Screaming Pelican. Haley pulls out a little box and pushes it across the table.

"I can't wait to see what this year's hideous ornament will be." Last year, she got us a sloth-faced Santa riding an ostrich. It was disturbing. It's also my favorite so far.

Opening the package, I freeze, confusion eating up my brain cells.

"I just found out last week," she says cautiously.

I gingerly pull out a little silver ornament that's the shape of a rattle. It even jingles.

My heart jams into my throat. "Is this what I think it is?"

"We're due in June."

I'm a clusterfuck of emotions. Tears fill my eyes, my hands are shaking, hell my whole ass body is shaking, and I can't feel my feet. "We're having a baby."

Haley tucks her hair behind her ears. "Are you happy?"

"Am I…" I can't feel my face. "Am I *happy*?"

That's not a strong enough word for this emotion. "We're having a baby." I get out of the booth, pull her out, too, and twirl Haley around. *"We're having a baby!"* I scream so everyone in the restaurant hears us.

Cheers erupt, and Haley tips her head back, laughing.

Setting her down, I cup her face and kiss her hard. "I love you so much." Gently rubbing my hand on her lower belly, I want to scream, cry, throw up.

I've never felt this excited before.

I can't wait to tell my family, our friends, the

mailman and anyone else I cross paths with.

I've got an amazing wife. A baby on the way. A career I love. A house I made. And the ugliest Christmas tree in the whole wide world.

I'm the luckiest man on earth and nothing will ever change that.

Haley and I built our dreams and found our way back together, just like we were meant to. And now we're going to start a new adventure together, just when we're meant to.

Timing is everything.

And so is Haley.

OTHER BOOKS
BY THIS AUTHOR

For information on this book, other books in my backlist, and future releases,
please visit: **www.BrianaMichaels.com**

If you liked this book, please help spread the word by leaving a review on the site you purchased your copy, or on a reader site such as Goodreads.

I'd love to hear from readers too, so feel free to send me an email at: sinsofthesidhe@gmail.com or visit me on Facebook:
www.facebook.com/BrianaMichaelsAuthor

Thank you!

ABOUT THE AUTHOR

Briana Michaels grew up and still lives on the East Coast. When taking a break from the crazy adventures in her head, she enjoys running around with her two children. If there is time to spare, she loves to read, cook, hike in the woods, and sit outside by a roaring fire. She does all of this with the love and support of her amazing husband who always has her back, encouraging her to go for her dreams. Aye, she's a lucky girl indeed.

56112762R00141